Pretty Freek

The Mystery of
the Mystery Meat

WITHDRAWN
FROM THE RECORDS OF THE
MID-CONTINENT PUBLIC LIBRARY

JF   MAY   2008
Flesh, Chris P.
The mystery of the mystery
  meat

MID-CONTINENT PUBLIC LIBRARY
North Oak Branch
8700 N. Oak Trafficway   NO
Kansas City, MO 64155

a novel by
Chris P Flesh

Illustrated by Saxton Moore and Carlos Villagra

Continued thanks to Nancy Holder,
who helped bring this story to life.

GROSSET & DUNLAP
Published by the Penguin Group
Penguin Group (USA) Inc., 375 Hudson Street, New York, New York 10014, USA
Penguin Group (Canada), 90 Eglinton Avenue East, Suite 700, Toronto, Ontario M4P 2Y3,
Canada (a division of Pearson Penguin Canada Inc.)
Penguin Books Ltd., 80 Strand, London WC2R 0RL, England
Penguin Group Ireland, 25 St. Stephen's Green, Dublin 2, Ireland
(a division of Penguin Books Ltd.)
Penguin Group (Australia), 250 Camberwell Road, Camberwell, Victoria 3124, Australia
(a division of Pearson Australia Group Pty. Ltd.)
Penguin Books India Pvt. Ltd., 11 Community Centre,
Panchsheel Park, New Delhi—110 017, India
Penguin Group (NZ), 67 Apollo Drive, Rosedale, North Shore 0632, New Zealand
(a division of Pearson New Zealand Ltd.)
Penguin Books (South Africa) (Pty.) Ltd., 24 Sturdee Avenue,
Rosebank, Johannesburg 2196, South Africa

Penguin Books Ltd., Registered Offices: 80 Strand, London WC2R 0RL, England

If you purchased this book without a cover, you should be aware that this book is stolen
property. It was reported as "unsold and destroyed" to the publisher, and neither the author nor
the publisher has received any payment for this "stripped book."

The scanning, uploading, and distribution of this book via the Internet or via any other means
without the permission of the publisher is illegal and punishable by law. Please purchase only
authorized electronic editions, and do not participate in or encourage electronic piracy of
copyrighted materials. Your support of the author's rights is appreciated.

Pretty Freekin Scary™ and related trademarks © 2008 Cloudco, Inc. Used under license by
Penguin Young Readers Group. All rights reserved. Published by Grosset & Dunlap, a division
of Penguin Young Readers Group, 345 Hudson Street, New York, New York 10014. GROSSET
& DUNLAP is a trademark of Penguin Group (USA) Inc. Printed in the U.S.A.

Library of Congress Cataloging-in-Publication Data is available.

ISBN 978-0-448-44811-4   10 9 8 7 6 5 4 3 2 1

Prologue:
In Which Your Beloved Narrator Exercises Remarkable Self-Control!

Welcome, Dear and Gentle Reader, to this book. I am Chris P. Flesh, Narrator Extraordinaire, and it is my extreme pleasure to completely unnerve you with the horribly thrilling and excruciatingly nerve-wracking adventures of Franklin Ripp. If you have walked the twisted, terror-infested path of Franklin's journey with me before, you know what you are in for. But if you are

MID-CONTINENT PUBLIC LIBRARY
North Oak Branch
8700 N. Oak Trafficway
Kansas City, MO 64155
NO

MID-CONTINENT PUBLIC LIBRARY - BTM

3 0003 00616735 5

new to this strange tale of an undead boy, the girl he loves, and his two best friends from the Underworld, well, then, I hope you have a strong stomach and a courageous heart, because you are going to need them.

But first, allow me to bring a ray of sunshine into this shadowy set of paragraphs: I am delighted to announce that the International Order of Narrators has agreed to reconsider their completely idiotic and highly unfair decision to throw me out of the organization. You may recall that I was booted because a VFI (very famous individual) complained about my curious nature, insisting that I had asked him too many questions in my attempt to narrate his story with all the care and feeling it deserved.

Can you imagine such a thing? I cannot. It would be like punishing a doctor for making too many stitches after he cuts out your diseased spleen (as well as any other rotting organs stinking up your abdominal cavity). Or firing a gardener for hacking down too many man-eating plants before the tiny Goldschmidt triplets arrive for an afternoon of mud-pie-making and insect-devouring in your backyard. As you know, asking questions is what a narrator *does*, and one certainly ought not be punished for fulfilling the requirements of one's chosen profession. For how can one provide information to the reader if one does not know—

A minute? This is Belle, the Narrator's

niece. It's kind of my job to interrupt Uncle Chris when he goes on too long. I'm visiting this weekend, and I brought my best friend, Haley, only I call her Elvis.

Hi! I'm Elvis, Belle's BFF!

Let me confirm that yes, Belle is here, and so is "Elvis," who is indeed her best friend forever. And interestingly enough, our new tale about Franklin concerns his two best friends *from* forever, otherwise known as the Afterlife. They are Scary, a shape-shifting phantom, and Pretty, a little monster who has two big eyes and five little ones, ponytail ears decorated with suckers, a mouth glittering with fangs, and tentacles instead of legs. They came from a part of the Afterlife called the Underworld, which is reserved for monsters and phantoms, and it's a good thing they insisted on accompanying Franklin to the Land of the Living. For they will help him solve the Mystery of the Mystery Meat, once and for all.

Mystery Meat, you may recall, was created by Horatio Snickering III in 1889, in a tiny kitchen in the equally tiny village he named Snickering Willows. Mystery Meat was an overnight sensation, and Mr. Snickering built an immense brick factory to increase production. The fabulous concoction was served to millionaires in the finest restaurants and to soldiers in the heat of battle. And it was served in school cafeterias across this great land of ours (and still is, to this day).

But its beginnings—and its contents—were shrouded in mystery. People wanted to know what was in Mystery Meat, and they bombarded Horatio Snickering with questions about his creation at every turn. *"What's in it? Would you please share the recipe as a favor to my dying nephew? Would you share it for a million dollars? Or perhaps in return for the lives of your wife, child, and sprightly little dachshund, Wotan, to whom I have become quite attached?"*

The questions swirled around him like the smoke from one of his ever-present cigars. Some say they drove him mad. Others say it occurred to him that while *he* might be immune to such a barrage of questions, others who worked for him—his employees—might succumb and reveal the secret recipe.

If any of Horatio Snickering's competitors learned how to make Mystery Meat, he would be ruined, and all his employees would starve. Literally.

So he decided that the only thing he could do was make all questions illegal, no matter how innocent or unimportant they might seem to those who asked them, or whether they related to Mystery Meat or not. It lay within his power to do so because, as I mentioned, he owned the entire town. If anyone was caught asking a question, no

matter the subject, the asker was charged with Curiosity, and if they were found guilty, they were escorted to the city limits and ordered never to return. In addition, if they attempted to communicate with their family and friends who still lived in Snickering Willows, those people would be forced to leave town as well. And they were never, ever heard from again.

Consider, then, what it might be like to grow up without ever asking a question. That was exactly what it was like for Franklin Ripp, who was born over a century after asking questions was made illegal in his hometown. He never asked a single question in his entire life, and he should have, because then he would not have died an early, horrible, disgusting, humiliating death.

(A note: I have promised never to reveal exactly how he died, because it is just so very awful that Franklin couldn't bear for you to know. In return, Franklin has allowed me to tell his story, which, while very dismaying, revolting, and stomach-churning, is nevertheless very juicy—just like Mystery Meat!)

I *can* tell you that he wouldn't have died if he had asked questions first, such as:

1. Is this dangerous?
2. Should I be wearing a helmet?
3. And a parachute?

These are only examples, mind you, because I don't want to give the slightest hint about the actual means of his demise.

After his hideous, disgusting, embarrassing death, he found himself in the Afterlife. He was most distressed, declaring his death "a total Ripp-off." His life had been going awfully well. He had friends, and more importantly, it looked like Lilly Weezbrock wanted to be his girlfriend.

A word on Lilly Weezbrock.

You might hear adults daydreaming about winning the lottery. "If I won the lottery," they will say, "I would quit this stupid job." "If I won the lottery, I would sail around the world." Kissing Lilly Weezbrock was Franklin's version of winning the lottery. He knew it would change his life forever.

He almost kissed her on the last day of school, but alas, he lost his nerve, and as I have noted, the next day he died.

Thwarted Franklin badgered the Afterlife Commission into giving him a second chance. He did this by asking the very first question he had ever uttered:

"Why? Why was I taken so early? Why did I come here when things were going so well? Why, why, why?"

Once he started asking why, he couldn't stop. The

Afterlife Commission got very tired of his incessant questioning. Monsieur DeMise, a member of the Commission, was a rotting corpse like Franklin and a romantic at heart. He suggested Franklin should be allowed to prove his life was worth living—by getting his one true love, Lilly Weezbrock, to kiss him by June 13—the end of the school year and, interestingly enough, the anniversary of his death. If they kissed, he could stay. If they didn't, he would return to the Afterlife and *never* ask the Afterlife Commission a question again.

Franklin agreed, and faster than you can say, "Rest in peace," he was back among the living. His parents were overjoyed, and his dog, Sophie, barked with glee and tried to bury his thighbone . . . while it was still attached to his body.

For you see, the Afterlife Commission neglected to mention that Franklin would come back as an undead corpse and that he would continue to rot (and smell) throughout the duration of his experimental return. As a result, Franklin's nemesis, Brad Anderwater, renamed him "Freekin," and the name stuck to him as surely as a maggot on a fresh lesion.

And so did Freekin's two friends, Pretty and Scary. I have already mentioned them. Let me emphasize that they were foreigners in Freekin's strange little town and

quite unused to (1) living (2) in a place where no one asked questions. And when Freekin came back from the Afterlife, he had also seen how good and necessary asking questions could be, since asking a question would have saved him all this trouble.

And he had a lot of questions about what was going on in Snickering Willows, because first of all, a terrible plague spread throughout the town. It was called Chronic Snickering Syndrome, and through skillful detective work (and asking a lot of questions) Pretty, Freekin, and Scary discovered that it was caused by a new flavor of Mystery Meat called Neapolitan Nacho.

Second of all, the people who made Neapolitan Nacho had also figured out that it made people snicker and snort uncontrollably. But instead of doing the right thing and announcing their enormous blunder to the public, they created another new flavor called Toasty Twinkle. Toasty Twinkle would turn anyone who ate it into a lethargic, uncurious sleepwalker who wouldn't care about anything ever again. Such mindless Willowites would buy whatever bizarre flavor of Mystery Meat the villainous Mystery Meatarians came up with next . . . yes, even if it contained broccoli!

This is Elvis, and may I say, "BLECH!"

Pretty, Freekin, and Scary succeeded in putting a stop

to the Toasty Twinkle plot, too. In a wild adventure of derring-do, Pretty set the Mystery Meat Ultra Top Secret Processing Area on fire, destroying the batch of Toasty Twinkle—and nearly losing her life.

So as we open our story, the factory is still on fire. Thick, gristly smoke clogs the air and fire engines barrel down the streets. Freekin has left Pretty unconscious in his room, watched over by Scary, while he races over to Lilly's house to make sure she is safe and sound.

Lilly thought Freekin was a hero. Frankly, I do, too.

And so do Belle and Elvis! Yay, Freekin!

And so did poor little Pretty . . . and yet, she will embark on a desperate course of action that may spell the end of Snickering Willows forever!

This is Belle. Holy cow! Like what? What does she do?

Well, my dear, if you want to know that, then you must read the book, like everyone else.

Hop to it, Uncle Chris. Let's get this story started!

This is Elvis. Please, Mr. Flesh, tell us what happened next! I am dying of curiosity! HA HA HA!

Very well . . .

Chapter One:
In Which A Kiss Is Interrupted

Freekin and Lilly strolled toward Lilly's modest, one-story house, holding hands and smiling at each other beneath the smoke-clogged moon. Snowflakes dusted Lilly's adorable nose and golden blond hair, and Freekin fell in love all over again. Their footsteps crunched on the snow, Lilly light on her feet like an athlete, while Freekin sort of walk-lurched, walk-lurched, like the Frankenstein monster. The heat of the fire at the Mystery Meat factory had melted the Wacky Glue that kept his left foot attached to his ankle, and he didn't want to stop and fix it. He didn't want to do anything that might break the spell that seemed to have fallen over Lilly and him.

The world was a muffled hush like the closing of a casket after a funeral. The wails of the fire engine sirens had died, and Freekin supposed the bright red trucks had all reached the scene of the terrible fire at the Mystery Meat factory. A fire Pretty set to stop the Mystery Meat people from feeding Toasty Twinkle to the town.

Go, Pretty, Freekin thought proudly. He planned to check on her as soon as Lilly was safely inside her house.

Freekin and Lilly reached the Weezbrocks' front door, decorated for the holiday season with an evergreen wreath covered with little teddy bears and red ribbons stamped in white with SEASON'S GREETINGS: THE SNICKERING WILLOWS MYSTERY MEAT COMPANY. Lilly's father worked at the factory, and Freekin figured he was probably not too thrilled that it was on fire.

"Well, I should probably go in," Lilly said reluctantly. She smiled at him, her teeth as white as finely polished knucklebones, her eyes as blue as oxygen-starved blood. "Crazy night, huh? I'm so excited for the Nonspecific

Winter Holiday Dance. Thanks so much for asking me to go with you."

"You're welcome, Lilly," Freekin replied, and his ears tingled as if they were stuffed to bursting with maggots. When he had first come back from the dead, he discovered that they fell off whenever he got near her, and he had learned to glue them to his head. He had learned a lot of things. He was really getting his unlife together, and he was absolutely sure he would kiss Lilly by June 13.

Maybe even now! he thought, thrilled to the desiccated marrow of his bones as they faced each other with her hands in his. Freekin took a breath, not that he had to breathe. But he was nervous.

Okay, here goes, he thought. He licked his lips in preparation of a life-changing experience.

He moved his head toward hers. His ears prickled and pulsed.

Then the front door crashed open, and Lilly's towering, muscular, unhappy father filled the doorway. Big and bald, he wore a pair of jeans and a T-shirt with the words MYSTERY MEAT UNION WORKERS, LOCAL 1313 stretched across his chest.

Lilly and Freekin jumped apart, and Freekin's left hand came off in Lilly's grasp. She made a little face

and hid it behind her back, and Freekin realized that she didn't want her father to see that they'd been holding hands.

"Lilly, you shouldn't be out tonight. Come inside," Mr. Weezbrock snapped, rubbing his large stomach. He glared at Freekin. "Hey, Dead Boy, go home."

"Oh, Daddy," Lilly protested. "Freekin's not dead. He's just . . . unalive. And he's a hero! He just saved us from—"

Freekin cleared his throat and gave his head a quick shake. He had explained to Lilly that she couldn't go around talking about how he had burned down the factory. He was trying to keep that a secret.

"Oh, right," Lilly said under her breath.

Mr. Weezbrock gave Lilly a death stare. No decent Snickering Willowite could ask a question, of course. Mr. Weezbrock couldn't say, "Saved us from what?" Law-abiding Snickering Willowites made leading statements and left them unfinished, waiting for the other person to fill in the blanks.

"Yes, he, uh, saved Deirdre and me from getting run over by a fire truck," Lilly said quickly, her eyes big and wide. "The driver didn't even see us! Freekin pushed us out of the way and let it hit him instead."

She flung her arms wide open as she gestured, and her father's heavy eyebrows merged into one thick, angry

unibrow across his forehead as he stared at Freekin's hand in hers. She followed his line of vision.

"His body parts went flying all over the block," she added. "I was just helping him find them."

"Humph." Her father looked thoroughly unimpressed. "You shouldn't have been outside where a fire engine could hit you in the first place." He opened the door a little wider and cleared his throat.

Wow, he really doesn't like me, Freekin thought as his ears stopped tingling. A large clump of snow slid off the roof and whumped the top of his head, breaking apart and covering his shoulders. He stared at Mr. Weezbrock, who glared at him with the laser-like eyes of an angry parent. If looks could kill, it was a lucky thing Freekin was already undead.

"Lilly," Mr. Weezbrock said angrily, giving his head a jerk.

"Okay, Daddy." Lilly gave Freekin his hand back. "Um, well, thanks again for saving my life. Good night."

"Good night," Freekin replied, holding his severed hand and trying to act natural as he stuffed it into the pocket of his jeans. The fingers stuck straight up, like someone trying for a low five. "Good night, Mr. Weezbrock," he added.

"Don't talk to me," her father replied as Lilly scooted

past him into the house. The door slammed shut in Freekin's face, and the holiday wreath slapped against the door like a floppy tongue.

As Freekin turned to go, he heard Mr. Weezbrock's voice through the door.

"That boy gives me the creeps. You should stick with Brad Anderwater. Star quarterback, rich, living . . ."

"Daddy, Brad is mean," Lilly replied. "Just give Freekin a chance. I'm sure you'll like him once you get to know him."

Freekin couldn't hear Mr. Weezbrock's reply as father and daughter moved farther away from the door. Freekin did the same, but his foot had frozen to the snowy porch and it came off with a pop. Sighing, he bent down on one knee and pushed it back onto his leg.

His stomach fluttered, a combination of lovesickness and maggots. As soon as he was out of sight, he plucked one of the little squirmy guys out of his mouth and set it gently on a tidbit of shiny green ham that had fallen out of a discarded sandwich he'd found.

"Party on, dude," he said.

People in love want everyone to be happy.

Freekin was in love, and Pretty was miserable. Tears spilled down her cheeks from her seven eyes and froze on

her face like random extra fangs. She chewed miserably on the telephone pole she was hiding behind, watching as Freekin strolled down the street with a goony smile on his adorable, lesion-covered face.

After all she had done, after all she had risked, her Freekin still loved Yucky Lilly better than her. Smoke rose from the top of her head, left over from the blazing fire she had created to save *his* friends and *his* mommy and daddy and *his* doggie from eating Toasty Twinkle–flavored Mystery Meat.

After working up the most amazing fire of her entire life (and she was over a million years old) to save *his* town, she had collapsed from the strain and fainted dead away. Next thing she knew, she was in Freekin's room with Scary bent over her, fanning her with his wings. Was Freekin there, pacing and worrying about her? Nooo. Freekin hadn't even waited to see if she was all right before he went dashing off to Lilly's house. Yucky, dumb, two-eyed Lilly.

So Pretty followed him and hid behind the telephone pole to spy on him and Yucky Lilly. She saw everything. The way Freekin's face lit up around Lilly. How he tried to kiss her. And how he asked Yucky Lilly to the Nonspecific Winter Holiday Dance. Pretty's heart was pulverized. There was nothing left of it, not even molecules, atoms, or electrons. Because she had thought Freekin had already asked *her*, Pretty, to the dance. In fact, she was so certain of it that she had spent an entire night gathering all the coins in the fountain in the center of the Horatio Snickering III Municipal Park to buy herself a fancy dress at the mall.

Had Freekin forgotten that he'd hugged her and kissed her right on the lips after she started the fire? That he'd said, "Oh, Pretty, I just love you"?

It must have slipped his mind. Maybe his rotting brain was breaking apart inside his skull, and those memories had tumbled into a sea of goo. Freekin would never lie to Pretty. He would never hurt her feelings on purpose. Or lie to her by saying he loved her when he was making goo-goo eyes, speaking of goo, at that *cheerleader* . . .

She took another bite of phone pole as she saw a light come on in Yucky Lilly's bedroom. It was Yucky Lilly's fault. Freekin just went all crazy around her, and Pretty had no idea why. Yucky Lilly had only two eyes, she had *no* fangs, just very white, tiny teeth, and she was completely lacking in tentacles. And still Freekin liked her better than the most beautiful ancient monster in the Underworld.

"Eat her eyeballs," Pretty grumbled, sinking her fangs into the splintering wood.

She tore out such a huge chunk that a crack shot up the center of the pole and split it in half. Both halves slammed against the sidewalk with truly impressive force. The power lines snapped free and sparked and danced in the puddles of melted ice on the sidewalk.

Pretty scooted into the shadows and skittered away on her tentacles, balling and unballing her fists. She didn't know what to do next. Maybe he had gone home, where she could talk to him . . . make him see that she was everything he could want in a girlfriend. Beg him to take her to the dance instead.

But a monster had her pride. Back in the Underworld, she had been very popular. Boy monsters lined up to ask her out. They brought her all kinds of presents to bribe her—fresh chunks of wood, large boulders, and delicately seasoned carcasses. Freekin just took her for granted. He thought she would always be there by his side, supporting him and cheering him on.

Well, what if she wasn't? What if someone else wanted to be her boyfriend? Then he would be sorry.

What Freekin needed was competition.

Her eyes spun. Her teeth clacked. She was on to something here! She would conjure up the cutest, most adorable boy monster in the entire Underworld, and *he* would be her honey-bunny. He would even be her date

to the dance! And when Freekin saw her all dressed up, dancing the night away with someone else, he would eat his heart out!

With renewed hope, she trundled on her tentacles through the stinging, icy mud as she skittered toward Snickering Willows Cemetery. She didn't mind the pain. It was worth it if it helped her get Freekin back.

"Okeydoke, me going for it," she whispered as she prepared herself to deliver a summoning spell. She gnawed for a while on a headstone, which put her in a zone. She smoothed her jumper and gave the little dead bunny head on the front a pat for good luck. Spitting in her palms, she slicked back her ponytail ears and pushed up the sleeves of her turtleneck sweater.

She took a very deep breath.

Her two huge eyes rotated like planets. Her five little eyes spun like miniature Ferris wheels zooming out of control. Steam rose from the top of her head. She threw back her head and in her best monster voice shrieked:

"AIYIYIAZEEEKOOTIEBOIIIE! SHAMALAMAHOTHOTHOT! YOOHOOOOOOOOOO!"

Flames shot from her eyes and mouth. The ice melted on the skeletal branches overhead and hissed into more steam. An owl shrieked, *"Wooooooooooohoooooooo!"* and

flapped into the night. The ground shook. Headstones shifted and fell backward and so did Pretty, right on her bottom, as autumn leaves showered down on her like colorful dead bats. They ignited, and Pretty's field of vision filled with smoke.

"Ha, Freekin," she whispered. "Ha ha ha." She blinked as the smoke began to clear, anticipating the arrival of the cutest boy monster in the Underworld.

But he wasn't there. Instead, she had summoned the rotten corpse of a grown-up human *man.*

Chapter Two:
In Which Miss Pretty Falls Under a SPELL!

Pretty stared slack-jawed and wide-eyed at the man she had summoned from beyond the grave. The moon shone down on his flaps of skin; the breeze blew the wisps of hair away from the shiny green and bone-white discolorations of his skull. Her two big eyes blinked and her five little ones spun as she noted the shredded striped trousers and the slime-encrusted vest, from which dangled a watch chain covered with moss. She recognized this man! She had seen a statue of him in the park and a painting of him in the library.

"You so Horatio Snickering III," she said, bouncing gently on her tentacles as she got up off the snowy ground. Her ponytail ears bobbed. She was very confused.

"I am, Miss Pretty," he replied, bowing slightly from the waist. His head began to topple off his spine; bone clacked on bone as he caught it with his left hand. Then he straightened and reinserted his scabby head onto his neck bone like a squishy pumpkin onto a fence post.

"And I am very grateful to you for casting that summoning spell," he added. "I used it to return to the Land of the Living, where I am sorely needed."

"Cute boy monster," Pretty protested, thrusting her hands on her hips. "Pretty wants!"

Horatio clucked his teeth—what few he had left. He was even more rotten than Freekin, which made sense, since he had been dead longer—a century, at least.

"Ah, sweet little lady, I have been watching current events from beyond the grave, and it has been driving me crazy. My fantastic original recipe Mystery Meat has been changed into something I don't even recognize, much less approve of. Neapolitan Nacho. Toasty Twinkle. Huge blunders! I've been turning over in my grave, I can tell you that."

"Bad Meat Men," she said angrily. "Eat their eyeballs."

"Yes." He sighed and shook his head. "Bad Meat Men indeed. I knew I had to get back here and fix things. And here I am."

"Oh," she said, nodding at him. "You asking Afterlife Commission, 'Please, one more chance, Ms. Totenbone, Monsieur DeMise, Lord Grym-Reaper'? They saying, 'Okeydoke, Horatio Snickering III! *Hasta la vista!*'"

He pressed his hand to his vest in a gesture of mild protest. "No, my dear. Unlike your friend Franklin Ripp, the Afterlife Commission did not send me back. You brought me here all by yourself. You are such a brilliant, amazing, and, may I add, beautiful little monster."

"Me so Pretty," she said sweetly.

"Indeed you are, Miss Pretty. You are a marvel." They smiled at each other, appreciating how fabulous and wonderful Pretty was. "Now I'll stop all this madness. With a little help from my brand-new, very special friend. *You.*"

"Me so helping?" she asked, astonished.

"You will be my very special little helper. Won't that be lovely?"

"Me so lovely," she agreed, eagerly nodding. Freekin would be thrilled! It would be like old times—like earlier that evening, in fact—with Pretty, Freekin, and Scary riding

to the rescue! Only better, because it would fix things once and for all—because of her! Because *she* had summoned Horatio Snickering III back to the Land of the Living!

"But let's think this through, Miss Pretty." He tapped his chin with his finger bones. "I don't believe the other good people of Snickering Willows are ready to see the founder of their town in my condition."

As he ran his hand down the center of his body, the knucklebone of his little finger caught in his dusty rotten vest and sliced the rotted threads apart. Pretty saw his rib cage and, in it, his heart, withered and unbeating like a dried-up crab apple.

"You see, I am quite undead," he finished.

"Freekin so undead," she argued. "Steve like Freekin. Raven like Freekin. Tuberculosis like Freekin." Her tone got edgy. "And Yucky Lilly lov—"

"I'm aware that Freekin is quite popular with his living friends. But you may also remember that he was tried for Curiosity, under a law I created. So I doubt that *I* would be popular with them. No, I think it would be better if I worked behind the scenes. That's where *you* would come in, my dear."

"Me comes in," she repeated fiercely, not at all sure what that meant. "'Knock knock, who's there? Pretty! Pretty who? Me so Pretty!'"

He chuckled, amused. "Something like that."

As he spoke, he reached into the shredded pocket of his vest and pulled out a shiny gold pocket watch. He held it up by the mossy golden chain, and he began to swing it left and right, back and forth, slowly, slowly . . .

"Shiny," Pretty said. "Watches at the mall. Happy holidays!"

"Yes, there is much to purchase at the mall for the winter celebrations," he said with a chuckle. "Like this pretty, shiny watch. Watch the watch, Miss Pretty. Keep all those lovely eyes on the watch."

She did. Soon Pretty heard a droning sound in her ears. She felt very . . . calm.

"Good. Very good," Horatio said. "Now you are under my spell. I have hypnotized you, and you must obey me without question. Say, 'Yes, master.'"

"Yes, master," Pretty murmured.

"Excellent." He grinned at her as he moved his watch back and forth, to and fro. "Now listen, my girl. I was able to see what you did to those two Bad Meat Men in my factory when you and your friend Scary escaped the chomping machine. You put them in a Terror-Induced Coma. It was quite brilliant."

Pretty's head swayed as she watched the watch. Her ponytail ears bobbed. Her eyelids began to close.

"Terror-Induced . . ." she repeated.

"Yes. You almost put Freekin into a coma like that once before. I don't think you realized it, and you stopped before you were done. But it comes quite naturally to you. And I want you to do it again."

She frowned slightly. He took a step toward her and cupped her chin, making her watch his watch.

"Listen to the sound of my voice. It is your master's voice. Do you understand?"

"Yes, Horatio Snickering III," Pretty said in a flat, monotone voice. "Me so understanding."

"Excellent. Now go back to Freekin's house and put him in a Terror-Induced Coma."

Pretty frowned slightly. She stirred as if trying to wake up from a bad dream. Horatio Snickering dangled the watch between all her eyes, which crossed.

"I want you to do this for his own good," Horatio Snickering said kindly. "You know how involved he gets in things. He's risked his unlife for his friends time and time again. I would hate it if anything happened to him."

"Freekin . . ." she murmured.

"I know that *you* would hate it if he were harmed, too, because you care for him so deeply. So if you put him in a coma, he'll be safely out of the way while I make everything better for him and his friends."

"You so good," she murmured. Her multiple rows of fangs glistened in the moonlight.

"Yes. I am very, very good. And so are you. You are good and obedient."

He put away his watch and pointed toward the rusty iron gates of the cemetery. "Now, go home and put him in that coma. And when I call for you, come back to me for more instructions. I will summon you with a special secret code to let you know that I want you. Like spies."

He thought a moment, and then he looked at the gravestone she had been gnawing on. Then he smiled. "The code words will be *Sweeny Burton*."

"Sweeny Burton," she replied, and something about that name bothered her. She tried to think about what it was, but she was too hypnotized. "Yes, Horatio Snickering III."

As she trundled off, something stopped her dead in her tracks.

"Horatio Snickering III?" she asked, turning to him with fear in her eyes. She was trembling.

"What is it, Pretty?" He sounded impatient.

"You so stopping the madness—bad men finished, eat their eyeballs! But then Pretty so hypnotized, forever and ever and ever and ever and ev—"

"Calm down, Pretty. Of course. I see your point.

We need an *out* word so that when our work together is finished, you can be released from my power." He scratched his head. "Let me think for a moment. Okay, I have it. When I say the words *the end*, you will no longer be hypnotized. Okay, my dear?"

"Okay, Horatio Snickering III."

And she left to do her master's bidding.

Still floating off the snowy ground with love-struck happiness, Freekin came home from Lilly's house. Scary was in his bedroom. Pretty was not.

"Where's Pretty?" he asked the little shape-shifting phantom.

"Wazeekiwakizi," Scary replied. He didn't speak English, and Freekin didn't speak Phantomese. Scary turned into a big question mark, then changed back into himself and shook his head.

"Hey, Scary, please be careful," Freekin admonished him. "I could get in huge trouble if anyone saw a question mark in my bedroom. Question marks are just as illegal as questions in Snickering Willows. And I don't ever want to get in trouble again. I just want to kiss Lilly and be a regular guy."

"Woodiwoodi," Scary fretted as he moved from the window to the mirror hanging on the inside of Freekin's

open closet door and changed into a question mark again. He stared at himself—Freekin saw his little eyes blinking in the center of the floating mark—and then he giggled and changed into Pretty.

"Wow, that's amazing," Freekin said.

Scary swirled his brand-new tentacles in a half circle as he turned around and waved at Freekin.

"Hiya," he said, mimicking Pretty's voice. It was incredible; he was a dead ringer for his best friend.

The kitties went nuts, rushing and tumbling toward Scary-Pretty like a river of fur. He changed into a Welsh corgi—one of his very favorite transformations, wagging his tail and licking the first kitty who reached him—Baby Tomato, the first cat Pretty had acquired and her number-one little sweetie.

Next he morphed into a bat and flew over to the window. He babbled something in Phantomese and waved a black, leathery wing at Freekin.

"Are you going to look for Pretty?" Freekin asked him.

"*Zibu*," Scary said. Freekin knew that meant yes.

"Okay, be careful," Freekin said. Scary blew him a little bat kiss and flapped away into the darkness.

Freekin picked up his guitar and strummed the chord progression for his new song, "Cheerleader Queen."

Then he sang the song he had written for Pretty.

She's a little monster, yeah,

But she's my little monster, yeah.

Calms me when I'm feelin' fears,

Has tentacles and ponytail ears,

She so Pretty.

He sang the next verse.

Her spinning eyes can freak you out.

Sometimes she rotates while she shouts.

Mess with my monster, I'll knock you out!

She's a little monster, yeah.

But she's my little monster, yeah.

She so Pretty.

After about half an hour, Pretty's face appeared in the window. Freekin brightened and put down his guitar. She had slithered across the branch of the old oak tree that scratched against the roof; it was the way Freekin and the monsters entered his room so his parents wouldn't see them. The Ripps still didn't know that Scary and Pretty lived in the house, and they also didn't realize that the dozen or so cats in Freekin's room belonged to a funny little monster who dressed them up and had tea parties with them. Freekin had asked if he could keep them, and his mom and dad were so glad to have their only son back from the Afterlife that they would have let him have a dozen boa constrictors if he asked for them.

He hurried over to his desk to help her pull up the window sash.

"Hey, where've you been?" he asked. "We've been worried about you. Scary went to look for you." He gazed past her into the darkness, through gauzy veils of gently falling snow. "Is he coming?"

She plopped onto his desk, then scooted down onto the floor in a tangle of tentacles. Her adoring kitties meowed and surrounded her, nuzzling her tentacles and chin. Usually Pretty giggled and picked up each and every one of her meowing little fur babies, giving them a nosy-nosy kiss that made them purr and bat at her ponytail ears. But now she ignored them as if they weren't there. Moving woodenly, she stood up and stared blankly at Freekin.

"Pretty, are you okay?"

Her eyes widened. Some of them began to spin clockwise. Others spun counterclockwise.

"Terror," she whispered. "Coma."

Pretty glided closer to Freekin, her arms stretched straight out in front of her body, her eyes spinning. Drool hung like a teardrop on the pointed tip of one of her fangs.

Chapter Three:
In Which Pretty's Spell Backfires!

"Pretty, what . . . are . . . you . . . do . . ." Freekin gasped, breaking out in goose bumps, his hair—what there was of it—standing straight up. His hands shook; his mouth worked. He had never been more afraid in his unlife.

"Pretty, stop," he begged, taking a step backward.

"Terror," she said again, trundling toward him. Her eyes became so wide that one of the little ones popped out

of its socket and bounced onto the hardwood floor. Two of the kitties pounced on it as it rolled beneath Freekin's bed.

"Pretty, please." Freekin tried to raise his hands to shield his eyes, but his arms hung limply at his sides.

"Coma," Pretty said in a stage whisper. "Wahahaha."

Freekin staggered backward across the room. His back hit the open closet door; his head rapped hard on the mirror he had hung so Pretty could apply her makeup and curl her ears. He tried to make himself dart into the closet and slam the door shut, but he couldn't move. Rooted to the spot, he shook like a death's-head moth pushing out of its cocoon.

Pretty's six remaining eyes pulled him under the dark sea of her gaze. Wave after wave of terror washed over him as she glided forward like a spiral-eyed, multi-fanged jellyfish of destruction, padding closer, ever closer, on her tentacles.

Freekin tottered; he opened his mouth to scream, but no sound came out. His teeth clacked and his knees buckled, and he began to sink to the floor like a drowning victim.

"*Gazeekeekiwoodiwoodi!*" someone screamed. It was Scary, flying in through the window. He took one look at Freekin, and then at Pretty, and zoomed in front of Freekin, throwing open his wings to shield his human buddy from his monster pal. He gibbered at Pretty, and then he started to whimper. He flew backward against Freekin, and the two tottered onto the floor.

Pretty's spinning eyes stared back at her from her own reflection in the mirror.

Her fangs clacked. Another small eye popped right out of the socket, and some more of her cats began to bat it around.

"Oh, oh," Pretty whimpered. "Me so terrifying!"

Her remaining eyes rolled back in her head and she fell backward with a crash. Her tentacles twitched once, twice, and then were still. Her kitties swarmed over her, purring and rubbing against her in sheer joy, unaware that there was anything wrong.

"Wakeekee meeka?" Scary cried. He flew over to her and tugged gently on her hand, and when that didn't work, he fanned her with his wings.

"Woodiwoodi," he fretted, giving her little butterfly kisses. She didn't move an inch.

"Pretty, what's wrong with you? Scary, what was she doing to us?" Freekin asked as the effects of Pretty's spell—or whatever it was—faded and he could move around again. Scary started chattering at him as Freekin got to his feet and hurried over to his unconscious friend.

"Pretty," he said, shaking her shoulders very gently. He took one of her small hands in his and patted it. "Pretty, talk to me."

Her eyes remained closed. She didn't move.

"Maybe starting the fire did something to her," he said. "Knocked a screw loose." He reached forward and lifted up one of her lids. All he saw was white; her eye had rolled up and her pupil was hidden. He released her lid and gave her cheek a gentle caress. Then he sat back on his knees and scratched his head. Dead skin collected beneath his fingernails.

"*Woodiwoodi*," Scary murmured, perching on Freekin's shoulder and wrapping a wing around his head.

"I know you're scared," Freekin said. "I am, too. We've *got* to find out what's wrong with her. She would never do anything to hurt us if she were okay."

The e-mail in-box of Freekin's desktop computer pinged, signaling the arrival of a message. Scary squeaked and instantly transformed into a brightly glowing lightbulb.

"You have an idea?"

"*Zibu*," Scary said, zooming over to the computer keyboard. He changed into a pair of human hands and began to type.

Freekin walked over to his study desk and looked at his computer monitor, briefly noting that the e-mail message was from his best human friend, Steve. The subject header was FIRE! Freekin ignored it and concentrated on Scary.

Scary had typed something in a font Freekin didn't

know his computer even had, much less that he could read, and in a second, a big smiling skull appeared on the screen with the words AFTER and NET written in crossed diagonal lines beneath its jaw, like crossbones.

"What's the Afternet? Is it like the Internet but for people in the Afterlife?"

Scary looked at him hopefully. *"Gazeeki walikikizu!"*

"Man, I wish I spoke Phantomese," Freekin said.

"Zibu," Scary replied, pointing to himself, which Freekin took to mean, "Me too." He pointed from Freekin to the keyboard and back again.

Freekin hesitated. "You want me to surf the Afternet? Is it allowed? I mean, will I get in trouble for using the Afternet in the Land of the Living?"

Scary whistled innocently. Then he slid his glance meaningfully in Pretty's direction.

"Right. I should risk it for Pretty," Freekin agreed. "Um, can I do it in English?"

"Zibu!" Scary clapped his wings together and pointed happily at the keys. *"Zibu zibu!"*

Freekin sat down at the keyboard. "Okay, let me think," he said, half to himself. "She was talking about something . . . terriers? Comas?"

He typed in the words. The skull on the screen whirled around in a circle, and then it stuck out its tongue.

"I guess that means no match," Freekin said. "Hmmm . . . tailors?" He typed in *tailor*.

The skull stuck out its tongue again.

"Gazeekee, woodiwoodiwoodi," Scary suggested, perching on Freekin's shoulder. He wrapped his left wing around Freekin's head and pointed at the monitor with the other. Then he shuddered hard and gasped. *"Woodiwoodiwoodi."*

Freekin might not speak Phantomese, but he did know that when Scary said, *"Woodiwoodi,"* it meant that he was frightened or nervous. *Of course.* When Pretty had stared at him, Freekin had felt *terrified*.

"Terror!" he cried. "A terror . . . coma?" He frowned and started typing.

T-E-R-R-O-R C-O-M

Before he could finish the word, the keys clacked out:

TERROR-INDUCED COMA:

Description Of

How to Perform

Cure

"That's got to be it, Scary!" he cried, moving his cursor to **Description Of** as Scary bounced on his shoulder and gave his temple butterfly kisses.

MOST TERROR-INDUCED COMAS INCLUDE COLD CHILLS, EXTREME TERROR, AND PASSING OUT DUE TO SHEER FRIGHT. UNDERWORLDER MONSTERS

ARE EXTREMELY ADEPT AT CREATING SUCH COMAS,
ESPECIALLY IF THEY ARE OVER A MILLION YEARS OLD
AND NAMED PRETTY.

"Wow, check it out," Freekin said as he read the
words on the screen. "Pretty is, like, the definition of
Terror-Induced Comas! Did you know that?"

"*Gazeelikiki waziliki wadiwadiwoodiwoodi*," Scary said,
very earnestly. As he talked, he gestured to Pretty,
then to himself, then to Freekin, then to the computer.
"*Kazeekiwalalilika*."

He went on and on, but it all sounded the same
to Freekin. Freekin glazed over until Scary threw his
wings around his own throat, making a strangling
noise as his eyes bugged out, then he fell backward off
Freekin's shoulder, sailing through the air and landing
with a thud on the floor. His eyes shut tight and all the
air in his small, square body escaped in a squeal.

"Scary! What's the matter?" Freekin cried, dropping
to his knees beside him.

"*Galeekiwazi booooooooo*," Scary babbled, lifting his
head and smiling at Freekin.

"You scared me to death," Freekin said, wrapping
his hand around Scary's wing and pulling him upright.
"*Please* don't try to explain anything to me. There's a link
for a cure. Let me try that."

He went back to the desk and scrolled to **Cure**.

He clicked it open.

TERROR-INDUCED COMAS ARE A FORM OF SPELL. IN SOME CASES THEY CAN BE CURED BY A REPETITION OF THE PROPER REMOVAL SPELL. BELOW ARE A LIST OF POSSIBLE REMOVAL SPELLS. THEY MUST BE SPOKEN WITHIN EARSHOT OF THE TERRORIZED VICTIM.

Freekin scrolled to large chunks of text in weird fonts that he couldn't read.

"Hmmm," he said. "Maybe I could point to the words and you could say them. You probably have a better idea how to pronounce them." He cocked his head as Scary stared intently at him. "Do you understand me?" He pointed to the computer screen and then to Scary.

"Zibu," Scary said, puffing out his chest and clearing his throat. Then he raised his wings over his head. He looked like he was preparing to do jumping jacks in gym class.

"Okay, try this one," Freekin said, highlighting the first line of wacky characters on the screen.

"Zibu," Scary said. He fluttered three times to the right, then three times to the left. Then he threw back his little head. What came out sounded like a cross between a wheeze and a snort.

"CANDI TAMALI DORICHEETO!"

Freekin crossed his fingers and looked over at Pretty. She jerked and quivered, shimmied and shook, then she transformed into a six-foot-long roll of what looked like jiggling, slime green jelly.

"Oh, my God!" he shouted, uncrossing his fingers so fast that his right pointer finger broke off at the base. Scary raised a brow and gave his head a little shake, as if Pretty's bizarre appearance was no big deal.

"Quick, Scary, try the next one," Freekin said, using his pointer finger to tap the next spell on the monitor. As Scary nodded, Freekin pushed his finger back into the knuckle. "**OTEEMCIROD ILAMAT IDNAD!**"

That changed Pretty into a dwarflike creature about a foot tall, with a very big head covered with white hair that tumbled over a squat body. She was dressed in a green shirt and green pants, and she had legs instead of tentacles. Eight or nine of Pretty's cats swarmed around her, yowling and meowing, and Pretty-dwarf opened two eyes framed by bushy white eyebrows. She sat up and laughed as the cats pushed her back down to the floor.

"Ach, da lina da lou!" Pretty-dwarf said, kicking her stubby arms and legs.

"Well, at least she's not in a coma anymore," Freekin observed.

"*Gazeeli zibu,*" Scary said.

"*Da lina lina lou da lou lou,*" the dwarf jabbered happily. It burped and then it passed gas, long and low and stinky.

"Ewww!" Freekin cried as Scary morphed into a large fan and blew the odor in the opposite direction.

"*Da lina, da lina lina!*" the dwarf said. It burped again and wiped its mouth with the back of its hand.

"There's one more spell to try. Let's go for it. *Quick,*" Freekin said.

Freekin pointed at the screen again, and Scary nodded, taking a deep breath and shaking his wings like an actor getting ready to perform a part.

"Franklin, dinnertime," called a voice just outside his door. It was Freekin's mom. There was a soft knock, and the door began to open.

"Coming!" Freekin cried as Scary transformed into a net. Flinging himself over the chatty little dwarf, he hoisted her into the air and carried her away to the closet. Cats trotted after him, reaching up on their hind legs and batting at the air as Pretty struggled and protested inside Scary-net, who reached the open closet and zoomed inside. Dashing behind them, Freekin slammed the closet door shut just as his mother came into the room.

The bedroom door opened, and his pretty, auburn-haired mom stood in jeans and a Christmas sweater, smiling at him. A few of the cats gazed up at her and meowed, but the majority of them trotted over to the closet and meowed.

"Hi, honey, Dad brought a cheese pizza home from Rigortoni's," she said. "Come and get it while it's hot." She turned to go, then turned back. Her nose wrinkled. "And I think you need to clean the cat boxes."

"I'll get on it," he promised.

"Dinner first," she told him. "Be sure to wash your hands."

She went out into the hall. Freekin turned around and tiptoed over to the closet.

"I'll be back as soon as I can," Freekin whispered. "You should probably keep her in there for now."

"Gagee," Scary replied.

Freekin sighed, hoping the phantom understood. He didn't even want to think about what might happen if Pretty got loose and his parents saw—or smelled—her.

His left foot flapped as he went down the stairs. As he crouched down on one knee to push the foot back on again, Sophie, his big, furry dog, clattered on her toenails from the dining room. She chuffed at him and panted happily. He gave her a pet. Then boy and dog went into the dining room, Sophie scooting beneath the table and Freekin taking his seat across from his mom.

"Hi, Franklin," his dad said pleasantly as he separated

a slice of pizza for Freekin and laid it on his white china plate. "I saw a flyer at Rigortoni's advertising for workers to rebuild the Mystery Meat factory." Mr. Ripp had gotten fired from the Mystery Meat factory when Freekin had gotten arrested for asking questions, and now he managed the town's most popular pizza joint. "They're going to work around the clock to get back into production."

"So they're not going to stop making Mystery Meat," Freekin said dully.

"Of course not," Ms. Ripp replied. "Mystery Meat is Snickering Willows's main source of income. I don't know what would happen to our town if Mystery Meat went out of business."

"Oh," Freekin muttered. That was bad news. He thought he had shut them down once and for all. He figured that now that they were out of the way, he could collect his kiss from Lilly and go back to being a regular kid.

A regular kid with two best friends from the Underworld, one of whom who had been turned into a white-haired, gas-passing dwarf . . .

Disappointed, he sat at the table and pretended to eat (since he was undead, he never ate), sneaking his dinner to his beloved dog, Sophie, who waited for each cheesy piece of pizza under the table.

"I hope you're all right, sweetie," his mom said, stretching her palm across his forehead. "It's so hard to tell if you're sick. You're always so cold, kind of refrigerated . . ."

"I'm fine," he managed. He had never told his parents what he had learned about Mystery Meat. He figured the less they knew, the safer they were from the evil people behind the plot to turn everyone into mindless drones. "It's just been a weird day with the factory burning down and everything."

"They said on the news that only half of it burned— mostly the processing area. The entire batch of Toasty Twinkle was lost. That's a real shame," his dad said. "My pizza customers were really looking forward to trying it."

"Um, yeah," Freekin said. "Bummer."

"That factory has stood on the edge of town for over a century," his dad said. "A lot of people are going to be worried about their livelihoods until Mystery Meat is back in production. It's a lucky thing I didn't go back." He gestured to Freekin's plate. "Have another slice."

"Woof," Sophie barked beneath the table.

But Freekin was too worried about Pretty to stick around any longer. "No thanks, I think I'm just going to hit the sack."

"Of course. You look tired," his dad said.

"Yeah. I guess I am," Freekin replied. His parents

also didn't know that he never slept because he didn't need to.

He took his dishes into the kitchen, forced himself to walk normally upstairs, and inched open the door to his room.

The closet door was open. And so was the window, where Scary hovered, anxiously flapping his wings as he stared outside.

"Scary?" he called softly. "Where is she?"

"Woodiwoodi," Scary said, whirling around to face him. He jabbed both wings at the window.

Freekin joined him. He peered into the darkness to see a small white shape trundling down the sidewalk. It passed beneath a streetlight and Freekin realized it was Pretty, who had resumed her normal appearance, ponytail ears, tentacles, and all.

"Cool! Did you change her back? Is she normal again?" Freekin asked.

For an answer, Scary flew through the open window and hovered above the tree branch. He waved a wing at Freekin to follow.

"Okay, let's catch up with her," Freekin said, climbing out the window.

Chapter Four:
In Which Freekin SINKS HIS TEETH INTO a Chunk of the Mystery

Snow fell softly as Freekin and Scary quickly caught up with Pretty. She stared straight ahead as if she didn't see them, and Freekin figured that whatever Scary did or did not do to Pretty, she must still be partially under the spell after all.

"Sween-y Bur-ton," she said in a flat, eerie voice as she skittered and scooted down the sidewalk.

"Woodiwoodi," Scary gasped, shuddering.

"What's that?" Freekin asked her. He looked at Scary. "Is it someone's name?"

"Sweeny Burton," Pretty repeated.

"Woodiwoodiwoodiwoodi." Scary turned a sickly green and wrapped his wings around himself.

"Is she putting a spell on you?" Freekin asked him.

Scary changed into a human skull floating in the air. SB AUG 31 BATCH 1313 was written across the forehead in dark letters.

"Thirteen-thirteen was the batch number for Neapolitan Nacho," Freekin ventured as the three walked down the street. Above Freekin's head, tree branches crackled with ice; a dog barked; an owl hooted. On nights like this before his death, Freekin would dream of having some kind of great adventure. But this was not exactly what he'd had in mind. "Is she saying that Sweeny Burton died because he ate some Neapolitan Nacho?"

Scary changed back into his little phantom self. Pretty began moving faster, her arms stretched in front of her like a mummy.

"Yes, master, yes, Pretty comes," Pretty announced.

"Who is she talking to? What's she doing?" Freekin asked Scary.

Scary changed into a copy of Freekin's desktop

computer, complete with keyboard. Letters in one of the weird fonts sprawled across the screen, but Freekin couldn't read any of them.

"Did you find another spell?" Freekin asked him. He pointed to the screen. "Is that how you changed her back? She's still acting very weird. What's up with her?"

Scary creased his forehead and gave his head a shake; Freekin couldn't tell if Scary was telling him that he didn't know or if he didn't understand what Freekin was trying to ask him.

"Does it have anything to do with Sweeny Burton?" Freekin asked.

"Sweeny Burton. Yes, master," Pretty said in a flat voice.

"Pretty, listen to me. 'Sweeny Burton,'" Freekin said, darting in front of her. He snapped his fingers. "Do you hear me? I'm saying 'Sweeny Burton.'"

Pretty ignored him, slipping and slithering on the icy cement. Her five eyes never blinked. Freekin remembered that the other two had popped out, and he hoped the kitties didn't hurt them.

At last the trio reached the rusty gates of Snickering Willows Cemetery, with its cockeyed headstones, angel statues, weeping icicles, and marble urns choked with frostbitten vines of ivy. They were hidden by the shadows, and Freekin dashed ahead of Pretty and Scary, craning his

neck around a privet hedge at the sound of a running car motor at the entrance.

Beneath a smoky beam of moonlight, a fancy black limousine sat idling. A bone-white hunchbacked man dressed in a black uniform and a cap held open the passenger door, and a strangely familiar-looking undead corpse in rotted clothes stood beside it, scanning the area.

"I guess she's not coming," he said. He sighed and pulled a pocket watch from his vest pocket. "I wonder if she was able to carry out her mission."

"Perhaps she's on her way, Mr. Snickering," the hunchbacked man said in a whiny, whispery voice.

Snickering! Of course! Freekin recalled where he had seen that corpse before—not as a corpse, but as a painting in the library and as a statue in the park. He was Horatio Snickering III, the founder of Snickering Willows, the inventor of Mystery Meat, and the man who had made asking questions illegal.

And he had been dead for at least eighty years.

"Master," Pretty said, coming up rapidly behind Freekin.

And Pretty had personally burned down half his factory.

"Scary, we've got to keep her from going to him!" Freekin whispered as he grabbed Pretty's arm and put his hand over her mouth. Her eyes narrowed and she struggled in his grasp.

"Mmmrrr," she said.

Scary turned one wing into a rope and wound it around her from her shoulders down to her tentacles. Pretty bucked and writhed, but Scary held fast, murmuring anxiously to her while Freekin kept watch on Horatio Snickering and his minion.

"Well, we don't have time to wait for her," Horatio declared. "We'll have to check into it later. My great-great-great-great-niece is waiting for me. Let's go, Viggo."

"Yes, Mr. Snickering," Viggo said as Horatio Snickering climbed into the limousine. Then Viggo, who had big insectoid eyes that pointed in two directions, limped around to the driver's side of the limousine and climbed inside.

The limousine lurched toward the street.

"Let's follow them, Scary," Freekin said. He pointed to the sky. "Turn into the super-spy plane." He knew Scary understood that much English. He'd become a super-spy plane several times during their most recent great adventure.

Scary paled—a good trick for a black shape-shifting phantom—then took a deep breath. With a grunt, he transformed into the plane and shot high into the sky above the limousine. He kept part of himself wrapped around Pretty, who sat in the copilot's seat beside Freekin. She was no longer gagged.

"Master," she said, "knock knock, Pretty is where?"

"It's okay, Pretty," Freekin told her. "We're going to take care of you. We'll free you from this spell."

"Horatio Snickering III," she said, "me so coming, master."

The sleek black vehicle drove out of the town, through a heavily wooded forest, and up an amazingly steep hill. At the very precipice, an enormous brick mansion loomed against the moon like a black silhouette cut from paper and then ripped apart and glued back together. It was seven stories tall, with chimneys, turrets, and gables protruding from the sloping slate roof like growths. Smoke curled from all the chimneys and swirled around a collection of ugly stone gargoyles grinning down maliciously from the corners of the rain gutters. Portions of the brick were choked with ivy, and beady eyes—they had to be rats!—winked scarlet-black as they scrabbled around, hissed, and squeaked.

Suddenly Freekin could hear what was going on outside. The sleek purr of the limousine. The cawing of crows. Scary's eyes popped from the control console of the spy plane and blinked at him.

"Good job," Freekin said to Scary.

"Zibu," Scary said.

The car pulled around in a circular drive and stopped. Viggo emerged and opened an umbrella. As he limped around to let out Mr. Snickering, the carved front door of the mansion crashed open.

"Uncle Horatio!" shrieked a voice.

A stick-thin figure posed in the doorway with its arms flung wide. It was a woman with white hair piled high atop her head, held in place with a jeweled tiara. She was so thin, she would put many skeletons to shame, and her face was coated with so much makeup that even Pretty, who knew little about fashion in the Land of the Living, might declare that it wasn't fashionable. A purple satin gown hung from her bony shoulders by thin straps and bunched around a pair of black-beaded high heels. She wore at least a dozen clanking charm bracelets on each bony, wrinkled arm and enormous jeweled rings on every finger.

A tiny dog—hairless except for a poof of black fur in the center of its head—peeked from around her. It began to yip incessantly and jump straight up in the air like a spring.

"Hush, Mortadella," the woman said. Then she turned her attention back to Horatio Snickering III as he came up to her and clasped him by the shoulders. Mortadella scooted behind her and growled.

"It *is* you," she said adoringly. "I would recognize those eye sockets anywhere. Welcome, my dear great-**great-great-great-uncle** Horatio. You're here at last; I've been trying to summon you for so long! Come inside. You'll catch your death."

They both burst into laughter. The woman scooped the growling Mortadella in her arms and they walked into the house. The door crashed shut.

Viggo turned around and limped back to the limo.

After flying to the rooftop, Scary landed gracefully and changed back into the gag and ropes that had been wound around Pretty. Freekin looked around and spotted the nearest smoking chimney. There was a square skylight beside it, washed clean by the rain; he crept over to it, gazing down to look into a room where a fire blazed cheerily in a vast stone fireplace covered with gargoyle faces.

The walls were covered in dark purple velvet decorated with black velvet half-moons, and the sofas and chairs were heavy black wood. Paintings of ferocious-looking men in turbans hung on either side of a stained glass window of a black cat standing in front of a full moon. On a pedestal placed before the center of the window, a marble bust of Horatio Snickering III smoking a cigar glared lifelessly into the gloom.

Beneath a glittering chandelier, a massive circular table adorned with a glittering crystal ball stood surrounded by six purple velvet chairs. With Mortadella growling in her arms, the woman gestured for Horatio to have a seat on one of the puffy sofas and reached for an old fashioned Princess phone perched atop an end table. She dialed a number.

"Viggo, come back inside!" the woman cried. "Tea! Make it snappy!"

"Yes, mistress," the whiny voice whispered in reply. "Snappy tea."

"Oh, good," Freekin said. "We can hear them."

"*Woodiwoodi,*" Scary murmured, wrapped securely around Pretty.

"Mmrrr," Pretty added, her eyes beginning to spin again.

The woman turned with a smile to Horatio Snickering as she struggled to hold her squirming dog.

"Thank you so much for answering my supernatural summons, dear Uncle Horatio," she said, sitting down beside him on the sofa. Mortadella scrambled off her lap and trotted around the table. "At last you are here!"

"I've sensed you calling for some time," he replied. "I had some additional assistance with my arrival tonight. In the form of a certain little monster named Pretty."

"Mmmmrrr!" Pretty half shouted.

Mortadella cocked her head at the sound. She curled back her lips and sniffed the air. Then she tipped back her head and gazed straight up at the skylight.

"Wait! I think I heard something!" the woman told Horatio Snickering.

"Move back," Freekin whispered, scooting out of the dog's line of sight. Scary copied his movements, dragging Pretty with him.

"Just the wind, my dear," he replied.

"Well, I hope your friend Pretty can help us with our problems," the woman said dramatically. "Uncle Horatio, we're in terrible trouble. Our factory has been reduced to rubble." She threw her hands above her head. All her bracelets slid downward, making a terrible racket. Then she slumped in her seat next to Horatio and buried her head in her hands. "We are ruined. *Ruined.*"

"Lay your worries to rest, Henrietta," Horatio said, patting her shoulder. "We are not ruined. Besides, I am dealing with the source of the problem. It's Pretty's friend, that young undead boy nicknamed Freekin. I'm sure you've heard of him."

Henrietta looked up from her hands. "No, I haven't. I no longer mix with outsiders." She gestured to the room. "Viggo and Mortadella are all the company I need."

"Well, if you haven't heard of Freekin Ripp, perhaps you should get out more. He's the cause of a great deal of our trouble. I've hypnotized his little friend Miss Pretty. I told her to put him in a Terror-Induced Coma, and if she has succeeded, he'll never wake up because I will never command her to bring him out of it. And with him out of the way, I will restore all as it was, back in my day."

She clapped. "Oh Uncle Horatio, that's such good news."

"Yes, Henrietta, yes! We will rule this town like tyrants! Men, women, babies, and rattlesnakes will cower at the very name of Snickering!"

"I knew it! I knew we needed you!" Henrietta cried, leaping from the sofa and throwing back her head. She raised her arms and began to prance around the room.

He held up a hand. "We must move with caution. I haven't verified that my little minion has completed her task. I ordered her to come to me tonight, and she has yet to arrive." He cupped his hands around his mouth. "Miss Pretty, Sweeny Burton. Come to me," he said in a creepy voice.

"Mmmmrrrr," Pretty said behind her Scary-gag. She shifted and struggled in Scary's grasp. Freekin knew how strong she was, and he put his arms around Scary, trying to help.

"Pretty, please," he whispered in her ponytail ear. "Fight against his spell."

Mortadella barked harder, staring at the skylight, then bounded over to her mistress.

"Hush, Mortadella!" Henrietta said, scooping her up. "It's probably a rat." She looked from her dog to her ancestor. "We have a rodent problem," she said apologetically.

"Never fear," Horatio Snickering said, putting his hand on her shoulder. Mortadella snapped at it, and he scratched her muzzle. "Once my grand plans are in motion, I'll buy you a new, rat-free mansion. My return will mean the end of all your worries forever!"

As if on cue, thunder rumbled and lightning crashed. Mortadella erupted into a frenzy of barking.

"Mmm!" Pretty said, and something in her tone made Freekin look hard at her. *The end. The. End. Pretty so remembering.* She began to rustle. *Him so Snickering. Him say "the end." Coma so "the end."*

Snickering didn't realize it, but with those two simple words, *the end*, he released Pretty from his power.

Pretty looked back at Freekin with her two big eyes and three little ones, her lids blinking rapidly.

"Pretty?" he said. "Are you . . . are you back?"

She nodded. "Mmfrrmm," she said behind her Scary-gag.

"*Grrrowfgrrrowfgrrrowfgrrrowf!*" Mortadella barked, struggling in Henrietta's arms.

Thunder grumbled and rumbled and rolled, and all the lights in the room below the three friends went out. In the darkness, Pretty tapped Freekin on the shoulder.

"Me so sorry, me so hypnotized, me so okay now," she whispered.

"Oh, Pretty, I'm so glad," Freekin said, gathering her close.

"Something is upsetting Mortadella," Henrietta said below them. "Viggo, go outside and take a look around."

"Yes, mistress," Viggo said.

"We'd better get out of here," Freekin said. "Scary, super-spy plane!"

"*Zibu!*" Scary said as he transformed around Freekin and Pretty, and they flew away from the mansion, loop-de-looping by the light of the smoke-clogged moon.

Chapter Five:
In Which Pretty Reveals a Terrible Secret!

As Pretty, Freekin, and Scary dashed back toward Freekin's house, Pretty flung her hands around Freekin's neck and planted a kiss on his cheek. Oh, she loved him!

"You so saving Pretty," she said as she finished crawling under his bed to retrieve her two little eyes. They were a bit dusty and she had to pick the cat hair off them, but otherwise they were none the worse for wear. "So very,

very sorry. Pretty tells Freekin and Scary everything."

And so she did, beginning with her rush to the graveyard (omitting that she had gone there to raise a demon boy for the purposes of instilling jealousy in her one true love) and her encounter with Horatio Snickering III. She told them about being hypnotized, which she clearly remembered now that Horatio had accidentally freed her from her spell by uttering the words "the end" while talking to Henrietta.

"And your code to go to him was 'Sweeny Burton,'" Freekin said as they arrived home. Scary deposited Freekin and Pretty on the tree branch, and they climbed into his room.

"Sweeny Burton, him dead boy box, no dead boy!" Pretty said. She grabbed Freekin's hands as she bobbed up and down on her tentacles like a jack-in-the-box. "Pretty sees . . ."

She didn't know the words for "earlier this month." So she bobbed up on her tentacles harder, like a pogo stick, and snagged Freekin's school calendar, hanging in the center of his Wall of Lilly—pictures of Lilly Weezbrock plus some crepe paper from one of her cheerleading pom-poms and a gum wrapper she had touched. The calendar picture showed Lilly and the cheerleaders—*Grrr, Lilly*—but Pretty ignored her rival and pointed to the calendar square marked MY TRIAL FOR CURIOSITY.

"Me going bone orchard, hello, Sweeny! But me no seeing Sweeny Burton," she said excitedly.

"You mean, you saw his grave, but he wasn't in it?"

"You so brainful," she said with admiration, tapping his temple.

Scary, who had been listening intently, changed into the skull he had shown to Freekin earlier, with SB AUG 31 BATCH 1313 written across the forehead.

"So . . . he died from eating Batch 1313," Freekin mused.

"Dead boy head, him in Mystery Meat factory," Pretty said. At the words "Mystery Meat factory," Scary nodded.

"His skull was in the factory? Why? What are they up to?" Freekin mused. "Maybe they did experiments on his brain to see how Toasty Twinkle would affect people."

Dear and Gentle Reader, you may notice that Freekin is asking a lot of questions. As I mentioned before, once he had died and asked the first question of his life—*Why?*— he had learned the power of asking questions. Asking questions was a very efficient method of arriving at the truth, and Freekin knew that the Snickerings were up to no good. He just wasn't sure what it was yet.

"Time for a chart," he announced, crossing to his

desk drawer and pulling out his pad of lined paper. He had made two charts in the past—one was on how to get Lilly to like him, and the other one had listed the clues he and his friends gathered on the cause of Chronic Snickering Syndrome—which had led to burning down the factory.

He got out a marker and wrote across the top of the chart:

WHAT IS THE MYSTERY OF THE MYSTERY MEAT?

Beneath that, he wrote:

1. Sweeny Burton: Who is he and what does he have to do with the mystery?

2. Horatio Snickering: What's his plan?

"I'll have to see if I can find out anything at school tomorrow," he said.

"No, no, no." Pretty put her hands on her hips. "Freekin is so coma," she reminded him, making her eyes spin. "Pretty so . . . so . . ." She searched for the word, holding her hands out in front of herself and weaving from side to side. "Me so yes, master," she said flatly.

"He thinks that you put me in a coma and that you're still under his spell?" Freekin filled in. "Is that right?"

"We *making* him thinking," she advised, dropping her act. "Him calling, 'Sweeny Burton,' me going."

"You mean the next time he summons you, you go to

him?" Freekin made a face. "I don't know, Pretty. That would be awfully dangerous."

"Freekin goes. Scary goes," she added, grinning slyly. "You so spyful."

"Of course. We could back you up. We're really good at sneaking around." He smiled at Scary, who smiled cheerfully back at him. Then his smile faded. "But I should at least warn Lilly and my friends to be careful. If Horatio Snickering knows who I am, he knows they're my friends."

"You so coma," Pretty argued, her poor, pulverized heart ground into even tinier particles. Everything always came back to Lilly.

"I'll check on her right now," he replied. "We know the Snickerings are in their mansion. So they won't see me if I sneak out in the dark."

Pretty sighed. She knew there was no point in arguing. Freekin was going to do what he was going to do.

"Okeydoke," she said grudgingly. "Us going, too. Us guarding you."

Freekin grinned and tousled her ponytail ears. "You're always looking out for me," he told her. "Okay, guys, let's go."

It was still raining as they flew in the Scary spy plane

to Lilly's house. Pretty had nothing to chew on, so she gave her fingers a nibble, then swallowed back her tears. From all seven eyes.

Scary touched down among some maple trees. Pretty stayed inside the spy plane, staring out at Lilly's modest one-story house. All the windows were dark. Maybe they had moved to China.

"You guys wait here," Freekin said.

He tiptoed across the brown winter grass to a window lined with snow-covered bushes. He knocked softly on it and waited. There was no response. He knocked again.

The front door swung open. Pretty's eyes got huge as Mr. Weezbrock stood in the doorway, dressed in flannel pajamas and a ratty old navy blue bathrobe.

"I heard something," he said aloud. In Snickering Willows, one could not say, "Is anyone there?" Because that would be asking a question.

Freekin ducked down into the bushes. Everything was hidden except his right leg, which stuck out of the bushes at a very weird angle. As Pretty watched, Freekin's hands snaked out from among the branches and yanked his leg **off at the knee, then disappeared** back inside the bush.

After a few more seconds of scowling into the darkness, Lilly's father went back inside and shut the door. The light flicked on in the window above Freekin's

head. Pretty saw two silhouettes—Mr. Weezbrock's and Lilly's. Lilly was sitting down at a desk. Mr. Weezbrock leaned forward and picked up something that looked like a laptop computer. Lilly stood up and followed him.

Then the room went dark.

After about a minute, Freekin emerged from the bushes and tiptoed back to where Pretty and Scary were waiting.

"I could hear everything. Lilly's been grounded," he reported. "She was IMing with Deirdre when she was supposed to be in bed. She can't use her computer or talk on the phone or anything."

"Oh, too bad," Pretty said, trying to sound equally sympathetic. Ha!

"Yeah, I'll have to warn her in person at school tomorrow," Freekin said.

"You so coma," Pretty reminded him.

"I'll be really careful," he promised. "I'll just find her and warn her and leave."

Then Pretty caught her breath. "Freekin," she said slowly, "Horatio Snickering, him saying 'Sweeny Burton.'"

"*Now?*" Freekin asked. "He's calling you?"

"To bone yard," she said. "Me going."

"Okay." He took her hand. "We'll be with you every

step of the way." He looked at Scary. "Super-spy plane," he said.

They flew within a block of the graveyard and touched down in a stand of trees. Then they grouped behind a tomb, and Pretty worked on making her face into an expressionless mask.

"Sweeny Burton." Horatio Snickering's voice carried on the winter wind. Pretty looked anxiously at Freekin and Scary.

"Woodiwoodi," Scary said, putting his wings around Pretty and giving her a butterfly kiss.

Freekin bent down and kissed her on the cheek. Her blank face lit up.

"Oh, Freekin," she said happily.

"Miss Pretty? Is that you, my dear?" came a voice.

Pretty looked at Freekin and Scary and motioned at them both to stay silent. "You so lay low," she ordered her guys. Then she took a deep breath, made her eyes go blank, and stepped out from behind the crypt.

"Yes, master," she intoned.

"So you received my summons after all. I'm pleased to see that you're still under my thrall. I was beginning to wonder."

"Yes, master," she said again.

"Because *I* received some very disturbing news. Another . . . *friend* . . . of mine informed me that Freekin Ripp was sneaking around Lilly Weezbrock's home not ten minutes ago. And he should be lying flat on his back in a Terror-Induced Coma."

Uh-oh. Hidden behind the crypt, Freekin traded a wide-eyed look with Scary. Horatio Snickering had a spy, too!

"No, master," she said. "Scary goes. Him so pretending. Scary in bone yard right this minute young man. Scary shows master."

"You are referring to the other little creature from the Underworld, Scary the shape-shifting phantom. In that case . . . Scary . . . Please join us," Horatio Snickering called.

Scary and Freekin traded another look. "You have to pretend to be me," Freekin whispered to Scary. "Like you pretended to be Pretty. You looked exactly like her."

"Woodiwoodi," Scary pleaded, shaking his head. He transformed into a pair of pouty lips and then into an arrow pointed straight at Freekin.

"I can't. He might realize I'm really me," Freekin insisted. "Then he'll know that Pretty's not hypnotized, and he might do something terrible to her."

Scary staggered, dizzy at the very thought of harm coming to his wonderful Pretty.

"Scary?" Horatio Snickering called out. "Are you going to show yourself?"

"Him so shy," Pretty said.

"You can do it." Freekin clapped his hand on the little phantom's wing. "I have faith in you, Scary."

Given that it was still raining, Freekin needed a moment to realize that Scary transformed himself next into a giant drop of sweat. Then Scary changed back, licked his lips and narrowed his eyes . . . and morphed into Freekin.

"Ta da," Scary bleated.

"Good. Show him," Freekin whispered.

Walking stiff-legged, Scary-as-Freekin stepped from behind the crypt. Freekin stood statue still, straining to listen through the rain, fearful of being seen.

"See? Scary so Freekin," Pretty said in a monotone. "Ha ha, big fat joke."

"I need proof. Scary, turn into a xylophone."

There was silence.

"We not knowing xylophone," Pretty said.

"Then . . . turn into a cat."

Freekin heard meowing.

"Very good," Horatio Snickering said. "I am satisfied. I should never have doubted a brave, smart, hypnotized monster such as yourself. I will continue

to use our code whenever I need you. Now off with you both."

"Okeydoke, master."

Pretty and Scary came back around the crypt. Scary wilted, bent over, and exhaled. He changed back into himself and Freekin patted him on the back.

"You so actor!" Pretty said, hugging Scary. "You so fooly boy!"

"You guys rock," Freekin told them both. "He didn't suspect a thing. That means I can go to school tomorrow and warn Lilly. I'll just pretend to be Scary, pretending to be me." He smiled. "Two can play at that game."

Pretty wasn't sure she understood. He wanted to play a game? "Tag? Scrabble? Computer game?" she suggested.

"No, I mean, sneaking around and pretending to be something you're not," he said. He grinned at her. "You are *so* funny."

"Me so Pretty," she reminded him.

"Yes, you are." He tugged on her ponytail ear, and she was more deeply in love than ever.

Pretty gave her arm a nibble. "Me no liking," she said.

"Don't worry, Pretty. I'll be careful," Freekin promised. "Nothing will go wrong."

This is Belle. Something's going to go wrong, isn't it?

This is Elvis. Yeah. What is it? I don't want any bad surprises. Can't you just tell us what it is so we don't have to worry?

Dear Belle and dear Elvis, your anxiety is music to my ears. It is the job of the Narrator to make you worry, and you both are clearly very wrapped up in my tale of woe and despair. I told you things would go from bad to worse. And so they shall.

I don't like the sound of that, Uncle Chris.

Me neither, Mr. Flesh.

Be brave, girls. If you are, you might get a reward at the end of the story.

What, Uncle Chris? Chocolate? Money?

Something even better. A happy ending.

Do you promise, Mr. Flesh?

Turn the page, dear Elvis, and let's see.

Chapter Six:

In Which Things Go From Bad to Worse!

In the morning, Freekin got ready for school as usual—taking a long shower (but keeping the water spray light so it wouldn't slough off too many layers of dead skin) and coating himself with deodorant to keep the smell down. When he had first come back from the Afterlife, he had worn his mom's makeup to hide his ghostly pallor. But he'd given up on that. He was what he was.

As luck would have it, the first person he saw when he got to school was Lilly, standing at her locker. She was wearing her cheerleading outfit, and she was so beautiful that for a moment he couldn't think straight. His ears tingled like crazy; lucky thing he had restapled them to his head that morning.

"Freekin, hi," she said breathlessly. "Come and check this out!"

She thrust a piece of white paper at him. Their fingers brushed, and he smiled at her.

He looked down at it. The entire page was one giant question mark.

?

"Lilly, what are you doing with this?" he asked, looking around. "You could get in so much trouble. Question marks are illegal!"

"Turn it over," she said.

Become a part of Generation ? Asking questions is GOOD! IT'S FUN! And you can learn how to do it! Come to a free seminar! Call this number to find out when and where! (131) 313-1313! The first fifty people to call are eligible to win a FREE HIGH-DEFINITION TV, A COMPLETE GAME SYSTEM, or A FIFTY-DOLLAR GIFT CERTIFICATE TO SNICKERING

WILLOWS MALL! Plus your name will be entered in a drawing for a FREE, ALL-EXPENSES-PAID TRIP TO THE SNARKSHIRES! Tell all your friends, especially your old ones. Generation ? rocks the house!

CALL NOW! (131) 313-1313!

"It was in my locker," she said. "I don't know how it got there, but I can't wait to go!"

"Lilly, no, you can't," he said urgently, crumpling the flyer into a ball.

"Hey," she protested, "that's my flyer!"

"You could be expelled for having this," he reminded her. "I don't know who . . ." And then he blinked. Could the Snickerings have something to do with it? That couldn't be. Horatio Snickering himself had created the law forbidding Snickering Willowites to ask questions. But the timing was . . . creepy. Could it be a trap?

"Good morning, Ms. Weezbrock. Mr. Ripp," said a voice behind Freekin. It was Principal Lugosi, the pale, baggy-eyed principal who had expelled him for asking questions—and made it very clear that he didn't want to let Freekin back in. If Mr. Lugosi saw him with the flyer, he would have the perfect excuse to expel him again.

Lilly stared in horror at Freekin. Before turning around to face Mr. Lugosi, Freekin popped the crumpled

ball into his mouth. He turned around and pointed to his throat.

"Errr, mmm," he replied.

"Freekin has laryngitis," Lilly blurted. "He was just telling me about it. Using hand motions. Because he can't talk," she added in a wobbly, nervous voice.

"It's probably another hideous contagious disease that he'll infect normal people with," Principal Lugosi groused. "Something he brought with him from the Afterlife." He glared at them both.

"Um, we need to get to first period," Lilly ventured.

"No, you don't," Principal Lugosi countered. "Your first-period classes have been canceled. I'm about to call for a school-wide assembly. I'll see you both there." He gave Freekin another hard stare. "Unfortunately."

Mr. Lugosi announced the assembly on the school's public address system. Within fifteen minutes, the entire Snickering Willows student body was packed into the auditorium. According to the unwritten laws of school, Lilly should have sat with the cheerleaders, who always sat with the jocks. But instead she joined Freekin and his friends—his fellow boarders, Hal, Otter, and Steve, and the goths, who treated him like a rock star.

"Hey, I got this flyer," Otter told Freekin. "If I go to

this seminar about asking questions, I might win some cool stuff."

"Me too," Hal chimed in. "Plus a free trip to the Snarkshires. I heard there's an awesome new skateboard park there!"

"Wait," Freekin said, "listen . . ."

On the auditorium stage, Principal Lugosi walked in front of a dark gray curtain the exact shade of Mystery Meat. He was carrying a couple of sheets of paper, which he laid down on a lectern in the center of the stage, and stared right at Freekin.

Freekin realized that he'd been caught talking. He tried to cover up with a fake cough, but Principal Lugosi simply narrowed his eyes and smiled even more sourly.

"Good morning," he said into the microphone, "although I'm not so sure what's good about it. I wish to address a very serious matter. Snickering Willows does not encourage illegal or immoral behavior, and if we catch anyone with flyers that *do* encourage such behavior, you will be expelled from this school and never allowed to return. And if you are caught going to any seminars that condone illegal activity, you will be apprehended by the Society for the Prevention of Curiosity and tried for Curiosity. Now we will sing our school song."

"They can't do that," one of the goths insisted as the auditorium filled with "Snickering Willows, Sweet Mystery of Life." "They're trying to censor our freedom of expression and take away our rights. They can't stop me if that's what I want to do."

"Me too. I'm going to call that number as soon as I can," another one proclaimed.

"Hey, let me see that flyer," a third goth hissed. "I didn't get one."

Freekin caught Raven's eye and shook his head. "This is not good," he muttered, trying not to move his mouth. "Meeting at lunch. The quad. Just us."

"Tuberculosis and I will be there," Raven assured him. The goths rarely ate outside—they avoided sunshine whenever possible—but Freekin had called the meeting, and Raven would do anything Freekin asked. Since Tuberculosis was his second in command, he would, too.

"Me too," Steve promised.

The assembly concluded and the students resumed their regular school day. Freekin watched in dismay as the flyers got passed around and people whipped out their cell phones—illegal to use during school hours—and called the number.

At lunch, Steve, Raven, Tuberculosis, and Lilly

showed up at the quad for the meeting. Steve explained what happened when someone made the call.

"You get a recording telling you to call another number after four P.M.," he said. "It's like a rave."

"That's cool," Tuberculosis announced, his coal-lined eyes glittering against his white face.

"It's not cool," Freekin insisted. "Don't you remember, you guys? I got arrested for asking questions. People who are found guilty of Curiosity are thrown out of Snickering Willows and they can never come back."

"You were found innocent," Tuberculosis pointed out. "Times change. I have *never* heard of anyone else getting arrested for Curiosity."

"Questions have never passed our lips until now," Raven reminded him. He cocked a black eyebrow at Freekin, the sunlight glinting against the indigo highlights in his hair. "You encouraged us to do so, dark wanderer. And now . . . you seek to convince us to stop."

"Because . . ." Freekin chewed his lower lip, debating how much to tell them. He wanted to keep them safe. "Listen, I think the Snickerings are up to something."

"There are no 'Snickerings,'" Tuberculosis shot back. "There's only old Miss Henrietta, and no one has seen her for years."

Freekin hesitated. "Please, trust me, guys. I—"

The hair prickled on the back of his neck. He had the sense that he was being watched.

"Go on," Steve said.

Lilly understood. She carefully turned her head to the right; her lips parted and her cheeks went pale.

"Principal Lugosi is watching us," she murmured under her breath. "Freekin's laryngitis just kicked in again," she said loudly. "Maybe you should go to the nurse, Freekin."

"He doesn't have—" Steve began. Then got it. "Right. His laryngitis."

"Freekin, you're holding back," Tuberculosis whispered. "We're your friends. You should tell us everything."

"Later," Freekin muttered.

He left the group and went straight home. What was he going to do? How much should he tell his friends? *Was* the flyer connected to the Snickerings?

While Freekin was in school, Pretty had been studying the picture of Lilly on his calendar, looking from the calendar to her face in the mirror on the closet door and back again. The poor little monster was truly baffled. She simply couldn't understand why Freekin preferred Lilly to her.

Was it her makeup? Her clothes? Pretty didn't know. She got out all her beauty supplies, which she had purchased at the mall, and applied a different color to each of her eyelids. Some were red, some were blue, some were black, tra la la.

When she heard Freekin's familiar walk-lurch, walk-lurch coming down the hall, she took a breath and gave herself one last look.

"Gazeekiliki?" she asked Scary, who nodded and blew her kisses.

Freekin opened the door and walk-lurched on in.

"Hi, Pretty, hey, Scary," he said, unslinging his backpack and setting it on the floor. "Something's going on at school. I think we should fly around town after dark, see if we can find any clues."

"Okeydoke," Pretty said, trundling up to him. She tugged on the sleeve of his sweater. "Knock knock, Freekin," she said shyly, turning this way and that.

"Okay, good," Freekin said, glancing at his computer monitor to see if he had any e-mail.

"Grrr," Pretty fumed, but she wasn't really angry. She was hurt. *How* would she ever get Freekin's attention?

Four hours later, the trio lofted into the air. Lightning flashed and thunder rumbled as the Scary spy plane

zoomed over the town of Snickering Willows. Freekin had expected the factory to be pitch dark, but super-bright lights hung down from towers, beaming over bright yellow earthmovers as they crawled over the rubble like giant insects and three large crews in hard hats and vests sorting through piles of debris. Among the workers Freekin saw Coach Karloff, his football coach, and Mr. Moulder, who owned the Wilting Fungus Day Spa.

Then he spotted a sleek black Mercedes-Benz emerging from the factory's underground parking lot.

"Let's follow that car," he told Pretty and Scary.

They sped high above it as it glided like a shark through the rainy town. Freekin's intuition paid off—the car drove straight to the Snickering mansion and pulled up to the entrance of the spooky old house.

Henrietta Snickering stood waiting in the doorway with Mortadella in her arms. The last living Snickering was wrapped in a black fur coat and a matching turban.

Two men and a woman dressed in business suits climbed out of the Mercedes. One man was tall and large; the other was short and trim. The woman had light blond hair that fell to her shoulders.

At Henrietta's urging, the trio hurried into the mansion. Scary landed, and the three tiptoed over to the skylight. Luckily, Freekin could see the two men and the

two women seating themselves at the table adorned with the crystal ball.

He listened carefully.

"Welcome, Mr. Flatterwonder, Mr. Spew, and the lovely Ms. Balonee," Henrietta said, seated in the chair in front of the statue of Horatio Snickering smoking a cigar. "I'm pleased you arrived so promptly," Henrietta continued.

"Of course we came as soon as you summoned us," Ms. Balonee assured Henrietta. Her voice shook. "Nothing could have kept us away. These are dark days for Mystery Meat."

The two men nodded soberly. "Dark days indeed," said the tall man.

"Have no fear," Henrietta soothed them. "I have emerged from seclusion to lead you with a brilliant plan to save our beloved company!"

"Grrrr-oof!" Mortadella barked as the three gazed at Henrietta with stricken but falsely eager expressions on their faces. It was obvious to Freekin that they were terrified of her.

"You three are Snickering Willows Mystery Meat's top executives, privileged to share in the secrets of our company," Henrietta continued. "Secrets that you must keep on pain of death. As you know."

"Yes, ma'am," said the shorter, rounder man.

"Good. Now I will reveal one more potentially fatal secret to you."

"Oh, how wonderful," the taller man said weakly, as if he already knew more potentially fatal secrets than he cared to.

"Yes, Mr. Flatterwonder, it is wonderful," Henrietta said. She cleared her throat. "Viggo, the screen."

ELIAS BYPRODUCT

Chapter Seven:

A CAUTION: THIS CHAPTER IS PARTICULARLY DISGUSTING!

As Pretty, Freekin, and Scary looked on, Henrietta Snickering's hunchbacked servant limped into the room with a remote control device in his hand. He pointed it at the fireplace; with a whir, a screen descended from the top of the fireplace.

Then the crystal ball in the center of the table made a half turn as its two halves opened, revealing a DVD player and a gray folder with the words SECRET PLOT written on the front in plain sight, dispelling any doubt that these people were up to no good. Freekin felt chills go up and down his spine.

Henrietta clicked on the DVD player with a flick of a long, sharp fingernail.

"The lights, Viggo," she said.

"Yes, madam." Viggo limped to the wall beside the curtain with the bellpull. He flicked off the lights, and the room went dark.

An image appeared on the screen. It was Horatio Snickering as a very young man, with his brown hair parted in the middle and pressed on either side of his head and a thick brown handlebar mustache.

"When my dear great-great-great-great-uncle Horatio Snickering first began creating Mystery Meat, he had an assistant named Elias Byproduct. A treacherous man."

The image of Horatio Snickering was replaced by a ratlike little man in overalls and a denim work shirt. He was standing in front of a little wooden building topped with a sign. It read, HORATIO SNICKERING MEATWORKS.

"After one taste of my uncle's first batch of Mystery Meat, Elias Byproduct knew my uncle was about to revolutionize the world of processed food. It was the

most delicious thing he had ever tasted in his life. But he was a terrible, greedy little man, and he made a secret deal with my uncle's rival, Frau Sausage von Meatschrapps, to steal the recipe and sell it to her."

The next picture was of a chubby woman with thick red curls all over her head, wearing a high-buttoned white blouse decorated with an oval locket. She smiled prettily at the camera and held a large German sausage.

"My uncle had never quite trusted Elias, which is why he hadn't shared the recipe with him. And so, one rainy night much like this one, he set a trap. He sent Elias to distant shores to buy more fermented fat. Which, as you know, is a very important ingredient in Mystery Meat. It is so important that a year later he built an entire factory, in the wilds of the Snarkshires, devoted solely to the fermentation of fat."

The three nodded.

"Yummy," Pretty whispered as drool collected on her fangs. Freekin nudged her, reminding her to be quiet.

"Back to my story. After about a week, Horatio wrote Elias a letter. He asked him to come back at once, because he, Horatio, had an emergency that required him to leave town. Of course that wasn't true. He was simply laying a trap. Then he left his cookbook open beside a bubbling vat of Mystery Meat and lay in wait for Elias to return."

Henrietta stroked Mortadella as her three guests sat at the edge of their seats, hanging on every word.

"As Horatio anticipated, Elias contacted Frau von Meatschrapps, and at midnight, the two snuck into the kitchen to steal the recipe. And my uncle leaped from his hiding spot and killed them both!"

"Eeek," Scary whispered, wrapping his wings around Pretty's arm and burying his face against her shoulder. Pretty patted him and kept listening.

"Then he thought he heard someone coming, so to hide the evidence, he dumped both their bodies right into the vat. And something amazing happened. Mystery Meat had been absolutely delicious before, but *now*, it was irresistible."

The next picture was of a can of Mystery Meat, followed by a shot of the enormous Mystery Meat factory complex in all its gory glory before Pretty had set it on fire.

"I never realized that's how he found the secret ingredient," Ms. Balonee murmured. "What a stroke of genius!"

"Yes, it was." Henrietta beamed at her. "But the real genius was that it wasn't Byproduct and Sausage that provided that extra zing. It was Curiosity."

"*What?*" Freekin whispered, astonished.

"Curiosity," Pretty whispered back helpfully.

"You must agree that those two wretched wrongdoers were *intensely* Curious about what was in Mystery Meat," Henrietta told her spellbound audience. "They were, in essence, asking the one question my uncle was so opposed to—'What's in Mystery Meat?' And it turned out to be them!" She cackled. The three executives jerked and worked their faces, but they couldn't manage to cackle back. They couldn't even smile. After all, the sole heir of the Mystery Meat company had just asked a question— and revealed a most bizarre tale of murder and mayhem.

"Since my dear Uncle Horatio had no idea that it was their Curiosity that made them so tasty, he made asking questions illegal in order to prevent the recipe from falling into the wrong hands. By his express decree, anyone who was found guilty of Curiosity was taken away by the Society for the Prevention of Curiosity."

The next picture was of a round-bumpered gray bus with small, smudged windows and large white tires. The words SNICKERING WILLOWS SOCIETY FOR THE PREVENTION OF CURIOSITY were written across the side in red letters. The driver was a stern-faced older lady wearing a gray cap with a red bill, and the bus was packed with unhappy-looking men in broad-shouldered suits, women in dresses and little hats with veils, and children in plaid flannel shirts and jeans with the legs rolled up.

"These were the good old days," Henrietta said. "Look how full that bus is! All those Curious people were traveling to our fermented fat factory in the Snarkshires to work day in, day out, for the rest of their lives."

The picture on the screen changed. It revealed a dreary, cavernous room packed with huge cast-iron cauldrons of bubbling fermented fat. The same men, women, and children, wearing old-fashioned prison clothes—black-and-white-striped pajamas and little round hats—stood on rickety wooden platforms, stirring the simmering goo with long wooden poles.

"And when *they* died, when they were stone-cold dead, we buried them in our graveyard. And when we ran out of Curiosity, we unburied them and added them to our delicious Mystery Meat," she concluded.

"Oh, yuck," Freekin groaned up on the roof. "This is so gross."

"*Zibu*," Scary managed, his little face twisted and distressed.

Pretty nodded. "Me so hungry!"

Henrietta's smile faded. "But now we come to Batch 1313. Neapolitan Nacho, the cause of Chronic Snickering Syndrome. The batch that nearly ruined our company."

The three shifted in their seats and looked uneasily at one another. "We're so very, very sorry. We don't know

what happened," Mr. Spew confessed. "We have no idea why Batch 1313 made people sick."

"I can tell you why," Henrietta snapped at him. "Due to my dear Uncle Horatio's law, the good, law-abiding people of Snickering Willows have stopped asking questions. In fact, most of them have forgotten how. And people who don't ask questions stop being Curious."

"Oops," Mr. Spew murmured.

"Oops, indeed," Henrietta said. "No one has broken the law by asking questions for quite some time. Even that undead Franklin Ripp was found not guilty! Today there are only *three* people working in the fermented fat factory."

She clicked to the next image on the screen, which showed the same dreary, cavernous building, but in place of vats, there were large stainless steel tanks. A very old man had his hand on a dial. He was dressed in a gray jumpsuit with the word PRISONER written across the back. Farther back in the factory, two ladies in identical jumpsuits were studying a clipboard.

"At least they're old," Mr. Flatterwonder observed. "They'll be available sooner."

"Yes," Henrietta said. "But you see the problem. We are running out of the very ingredient that makes Mystery Meat so tasty. And *you* people tried to cut corners by

using a corpse from our very own graveyard—that boy, Sweeny Burton. Think about it. If he was buried in *our* graveyard, he could not possibly be Curious. The Curious are kicked *out* of Snickering Willows."

Ms. Balonee nodded thoughtfully. "I see. We can only use the remains of Curious people."

"Indeed," Henrietta replied.

"But we're running out of Curious people," Ms. Balonee went on.

"Keep going," Henrietta urged her.

"So we need to rekindle Curiosity in our citizenry," Ms. Balonee said triumphantly. "No Curiosity, no Mystery Meat!"

"Exactly!" Henrietta cried. Her bracelets clacked and jangled as she clapped.

Mr. Spew looked a little queasy. "You're talking about encouraging Snickering Willowites to break our most basic law."

"Yes," Henrietta declared. "Precisely."

Mr. Flatterwonder looked even queasier. "We could change the law. If we explain . . ."

"*Explain!* We cannot explain!" Henrietta declared.

"Or maybe we could make a new ad campaign," Mr. Flatterwonder said, raising his brows. He stretched out his arms. "'Curiosity! It's not just for convicted felons anymore! Go ahead, ask a question! And have some Mystery Meat!'"

"No, you moron!" Henrietta thundered. "You haven't been listening. You can*not* connect our company with asking questions! I don't want anyone to be Curious about why *we* want them to be Curious. Imagine the uproar if people realize they're eating postmortem Curiosity when they sit down to a nice heaping bowl of Mystery Meatios."

"Yes, of course," Mr. Flatterwonder murmured, looking embarrassed. "I should have realized."

"We could be sneaky and underhanded," Ms. Balonee suggested. "We could make asking questions rebellious, trendy, and daring! Like . . . like extreme sports!"

"Yes!" Mr. Spew cried. "First we'll tempt the young people to ask questions. Then their parents will start asking questions. And then their grandparents will start asking questions. That's the way new trends always start—with the young."

"And there you have it," Henrietta declared. "I have already begun such a plan." She beamed at each in turn. "Look!" With a flourish, she opened the folder marked SECRET PLOT and picked up the first piece of paper on a small stack. It was a copy of the flyer Freekin had seen at school. She handed it to Ms. Balonee, then handed two more copies to the men. All three began reading avidly.

"Oh, no," Freekin murmured. "They're behind it, just like I thought."

"Smarty boy." Pretty petted him.

"Why . . . why, this is genius!" Mr. Spew said, reading his copy. "Forbidden fruit is always the tastiest. My hat is off to you, Miss Snickering."

"You take my breath away. Not literally, of course," Mr. Flatterwonder added hastily.

"I especially like the part about winning a free trip to the Snarkshires," Ms. Balonee commented. "It's a wonderful bit of irony."

"It's a lie," Freekin whispered fiercely. "All of it."

"Make sure these flyers get passed out all over town," Henrietta said, snapping her fingers. Viggo came into the room, carrying a stack of flyers that reached just below his nose. "Then we'll arrange a meeting . . . and spring our trap."

Within minutes, the three executives left the mansion with their enormous piles of flyers. Once they had driven away, the rotting corpse of Horatio Snickering III walked from behind the curtain with the bellpull. Mortadella barked at him as he smiled at his niece and clapped.

"*Brava!*" he cried. "Well done, my dear. You're a credit to the glorious name of Snickering."

"Thank you, Uncle Horatio," she replied.

"Now all we have to do is fan the flames of Curiosity and wait for someone to keel over," he said.

"I hope someone really old starts asking questions right away," Henrietta said. "No one will ever realize just how close we came to shutting our doors. We'll go worldwide with this! We'll sell Mystery Meat all over the globe!"

They both threw back their heads and laughed. Mortadella barked and licked Henrietta's face.

"Viggo!" she shouted, pulling the bell rope. "Bring us some blood orange soda. And some ladyfingers. We wish to celebrate!"

"Oh, my God," Freekin whispered. "They're going to eat some lady's fingers!"

The limping, goggle-eyed hunchback shuffled into the room with a silver tray. On it sat two crystal goblets filled with frothy orange liquid and a plate of rectangular cookies.

"Whew, they're not real," Freekin said.

"Maybe lady's in batter," Pretty observed.

"A toast. To Curiosity!" Horatio Snickering decreed, taking a glass and raising it high.

"To Curiosity!" Henrietta cried, clinking her goblet with his. Mortadella barked gleefully in her arms.

Freekin made a face as the two guzzled down their soda, then threw their goblets against the fireplace. The glasses shattered into a thousand pieces.

The Snickerings devoured their cookies. Henrietta set down the plate and Mortadella gobbled up the crumbs. Viggo returned with a dustpan and swept up the shards, disappearing back around the curtain.

Henrietta yawned. "Pardon me, Uncle," she said. "It's been a very long day." She smiled at him. "A long and wonderful day."

"Indeed, my dear. I'm very proud of you," Horatio told her. "Since you're not undead, you need your rest. You go off to bed, Henrietta, while I continue to plot and plan."

"Good night, Uncle Horatio," she told him, stroking Mortadella's strange little head. Then she left, and he sat down on the sofa and lit a cigar.

"Bad man, bad lady." Pretty balled her fists. Her fangs clacked. "Eat their eyeballs. Eat their brains!" She began to gnaw on the side of the chimney.

"We have to stop them," Freekin agreed, straightening up. "We have to warn people not to awaken their Curiosity or they'll be shipped off to the fermented fat factory for the rest of their lives. And after they die . . ." He took a breath. It was too horrible for him say.

Pretty tenderly patted Freekin's arm while Scary fluttered onto his shoulder and gave him butterfly kisses on his cheek. Freekin managed a weak smile as he took Pretty's hand and they walked across the sloping roof.

He put his arm around Scary's wings. "You guys are my best friends," he said. "We're in this together, right?"

"Oh, Freekin," Pretty breathed. "Scary so best friend, Pretty so bester friend." She kissed the back of his hand and laid her cheek against it, cooing.

Of course they were in it together. Pretty still had hope that she would win Freekin's unbeating heart. There was nothing she wouldn't do to help her Freekin.

Even if it killed her!

Chapter Eight:
In Which Freekin
Rallies the Troops!

"You needing cell phone," Pretty chastised Freekin the next day as he got ready to leave for school. "Pretty and Scary spying, 'Hello, Freekin! Waddup, dude!'"

"Yes, it would be easier if you could call me up to tell me what you've discovered while you're checking out the town," he translated. "But I don't have one."

"Me buying you," she informed him. She tottered over

to her little ruffled purse and dragged it behind herself on the floor as if it weighed as much as a bowling ball. She had decorated it with stickers of skulls and roses. Bending down, she unzipped it, and glittering silver coins spilled out.

He shook his head. "Did you take those from the fountain again?"

Pretty nodded.

"Are there any left?"

"No," she said proudly.

"Okay, well, be careful. Don't let anybody see you spying," he told her. "We'll meet here after school."

"Okeydoke. Me so extra-special helper." She fluttered her lashes at him. "Extra-super-duper!"

"You are. Scary too," Freekin said, smiling at the little phantom. "Later."

As the days passed, Freekin prepared for his fight against the Snickerings. He took Pretty's money and bought himself a cell phone. He silently observed the rising excitement swirling around him at school. Something needed to be done sooner rather than later. The illegal flyers were everywhere—sticking out of lockers, wadded up in the trash cans, fluttering along in the wintry breeze. Even his friends were curious about joining Generation ?

Freekin called another meeting at lunch. Aware that

Principal Lugosi might be lingering nearby, he had brought a clipboard and some paper so that he wouldn't have to talk. He wrote down his first sentence and handed the clipboard to Lilly to read it aloud.

Lilly cleared her throat and began.

The Mystery Meat people are trying to lure kids into asking questions so they'll be Curious.

"They want to help us," Lilly said, looking up from the clipboard. She handed it back to Freekin. "Snickering Willows is behind the times. We have to catch up to the rest of the world."

Freekin shook his head, wrote something else, and handed it back to her.

No. It's because Curiosity is the Ultra Top Secret Ingredient in Mystery Meat.

He gazed at their blank expressions.

"I don't understand," Lilly said. "Curiosity isn't an ingredient in anything. *People* are Curious, not . . . cows or chickens or . . . *oh, no.*"

Lilly sat down hard on the grass as if her legs had turned to rubber. She gazed up in horror at Freekin. "You can't mean that they're turning *people* into Mystery Meat."

Yes. That's exactly what I mean. After Curious people die, they become the number one Ultra Top Secret Ingredient.

There was a long, dead silence as everyone processed

that. One by one, looking green and panicky, the others joined Lilly on the grass.

"I *knew* I should have stayed a vegetarian," Lilly whispered hoarsely.

"You have to be wrong," Steve insisted. "That's just way too gross to be true. You must have read a hoax off the Internet or something."

Freekin hesitated. Then he wrote again.

I overheard a secret meeting Henrietta Snickering was having with some of the big shots from the Mystery Meat factory. They're the ones behind this "secret movement" to get people to ask questions. They want people to get Curious again. Because Curiosity is dying out.

"And it's dying out because we don't ask questions anymore," Tuberculosis said.

Right. That's why everyone got sick from eating Neapolitan Nacho. Because it was made from the ground-up corpse of some kid named Sweeny Burton, who didn't have a Curious bone in his body.

"I don't remember a kid named Sweeny Burton," Tuberculosis said.

"Sweeny Burton," Steve said, looking ill. "*I* remember him. He never did any homework. He never participated in class. His parents started home-schooling him about three years ago. I thought they moved."

"I guess the home-schooling didn't work for him, either," Lilly said weakly.

"There must be a plan to counteract this foul scheme," Raven insisted, doubling his fists and pressing his black lips together. "We stand at the ready to carry it out, pale wanderer."

"Yes," Lilly said. "Tell us what to do, Freekin."

His love for Lilly filled his chest, almost like oxygen. Admiration pulsed through his withered circulation system. She was so brave. She knew what was at steak— er, *stake*—and she was still willing to get involved. They all were.

He took the clipboard back and wrote in very large letters:

You do nothing.

"No way," Steve insisted. "We're going to help you."

He looked at his best friends. Correction: his best *human* friends.

Just act normal. Act like you don't know any of this. I've got some . . . help. Secret help. My secret helpers and I will deal with this. Just don't ask any questions . . . so to speak, until this is over.

"You're crazy," Steve said. At shushes from the others, he lowered his voice. "You don't have any 'secret helpers.' You're just trying to keep us out of this. *We're* your friends.

We can't stand back and let you risk your . . . unlife . . . without helping you!"

This time, Freekin didn't write down what he wanted to say. He had to make sure they were listening to him.

"The best thing you can do to help me is to stay out of my way. Just let me handle it," Freekin whispered. "And take my cell phone number just in case."

He recited his number to his friends. They all looked back at him, stone-faced. Finally Steve nodded. Then Raven and Tuberculosis, and finally Lilly.

"Thanks, guys," he said, but he had a feeling that things were going to get worse before they got better.

And so did Lilly.

She thought Freekin was really cool, but she also thought he was wrong. She knew he didn't have any "secret friends" to help him fight the Mystery Meat people. He was just saying that to keep her and his other friends from trying to help him—because he wanted to keep them safe. As usual, he wasn't thinking about himself. But what kind of a friend—a girlfriend—would she be if she didn't help?

So even though she had agreed to back off, she didn't. She had a great plan. By calling the number on the flyer and following the directions to keep calling back at

different times, she had discovered the location where the seminar was to be held. It was at nine o'clock that very night—a week after she had found the first flyer in her locker.

It was going to be held in the basement of the Horatio Snickering Memorial Library. And she was going to go. Then, just before the seminar started, she was going to stand up and tell everybody exactly what was going on. Then they would leave, of course. She, Lilly, would save the day!

As a chilly breeze whipped Lilly's ponytail against her cheek, she saw her best friend, Deirdre, hurrying toward the basement entrance of the Horatio Snickering Memorial Library. It was five to nine and, under cover of darkness, kids were swarming inside. Lilly saw Molly and Janeece, two of the other cheerleaders on the squad, as well as football players Brian Vernia, Sam Sontgerath, and Jesse Greenfield.

"Hey, wait up," Lilly cried, rushing up to Deirdre.

"Wow," Deirdre breathed. "Everyone is here."

"Good," Lilly said, half to herself. Kids swarmed around them through the door, which was propped open. "Listen, Deirdre, I've been trying to call you—"

"I know. I'm sorry I didn't get back to you. I've been

calling number after number to find out where the seminar was going to be held."

"I wanted to warn you that this is a trick," Lilly continued.

"Tish!" Deirdre cried, waving her hands above her head. "Look, there's Tish!"

Halfway down the stairs, Tish stopped and waved.

Lilly realized there was no way she could get through to anyone right now. She'd have to wait until they sat down and calmed down.

So she went inside.

Her eyes widened and her mouth formed a perfect O. In the far corner, a portable stage had been erected, with rows and rows of chairs lined up before it. An overhead sign read **WELCOME TO THE ? GENERATION!**

A very skinny, very old lady wearing a black cape was standing on the stage behind a lectern. A handwritten sign on the front of the lectern said, **CURIOSITY IS GOOD**. A goggle-eyed hunchbacked man stood in front of a whiteboard with a pointer laid across his chest. And on the other side of the whiteboard there was a life-size cardboard cutout of Freekin! It was labeled **FRANKLIN RIPP: OUR GLORIOUS FOUNDER.**

"No way," Lilly breathed, shaking her head. "That's not true."

"It makes perfect sense. I can't believe he didn't tell you," Deirdre said, grabbing Lilly's hands and scanning the crowd. "There he is! No, sorry, that's one of those goth kids."

Lilly shook her arms to make Deirdre let go of her. "You're so wrong. Freekin wouldn't have anything to do with something like this. Think about it. His father got *fired* from his job because of Freekin's trial, and Freekin got expelled. They're trying to make him look bad because they want you to ask questions!"

Just then, the old lady tapped one long, sticklike finger against the microphone. Feedback made the sound system squeal.

"Good evening," she said. "Welcome to the seminar. What a nice big crowd of Curiosity seekers! We're so glad you're here. Please find a chair and we'll begin in one minute."

The crowd—nearly all kids around Lilly's age—hurried to chairs and sat down. Then the old lady and the hunchbacked man left the stage.

Here was her chance. Lilly stayed standing and raised her hands over her head. "Listen, people," she began.

But no one paid her the slightest bit of attention.

"Deirdre! Janeece! Molly! Tish!" she yelled in her best

cheerleader's voice. "This is a trick! The Mystery Meat people are trying to get us to ask questions because they need people to be Curious again!"

"Curiosity is good!" Sam Sontgerath shouted back at her.

There was laughter.

"No, it's not! Not today. I'm serious!" she shouted, but people were hooting and laughing at her.

This is terrible, she thought. She whipped out her cell phone and dialed Freekin's brand-new cell phone. She couldn't even hear the ring, so she hurried out of the basement and tried again.

Behind her, in the basement, there was chanting.

"HOW ARE YOU?"

Oh, no, it's starting, Lilly thought. *They're going to learn how to ask questions. What can I do?* She gasped, realizing she had just asked a question.

She wasn't sure she was connected, but she took her chances. "Freekin, I'm at the question-asking thingie, and I need you to call me back as soon as you can!"

"WHAT TIME IS IT?" the group yelled.

I have to stop this; I have to, she thought, rushing back to the door. She peered inside. The hunchbacked man stood on the stage, and a list of questions was written on the whiteboard behind him. They included:

HOW ARE YOU?
WHAT TIME IS IT?
WHAT IS YOUR NAME?
WHERE IS THE BATHROOM?
HOW MUCH DOES THIS COST?
WILL THIS BE ON THE TEST?

She listened to them going down the list. She could just *feel* her own Curiosity awakening. It was . . . forbidden. Exciting.

And illegal.

She stirred herself. She had to break this up, *now*.

Then, just as she was about to reenter the basement, someone behind her grabbed her arm. It was Brad.

"Lilly!" he cried. "You have to get out of here *now*. The Society for the Prevention of Curiosity is on their way!"

"What?" Her mouth dropped open. She had asked a question. She could feel even more Curiosity surging through her bloodstream. "And what are *you* doing here?"

"Shhh, don't do that," he said, grimacing. Then he lowered his voice. "I called the number on the flyer, just like everybody else. I was . . . kind of Curious, I admit it." He looked very embarrassed. "I was on my way over here, and I saw the bus coming. I was going to just leave, but then I saw you and I knew I had to warn you. We have to go now!"

"What bus?" She winced. *Another* question! More Curiosity!

"It's the bus for the Society of the Prevention of Curiosity. It's almost here!" He turned and pointed. "They'll arrest us, just like Principal Lugosi said."

Sure enough, a big lumbering bus was rolling down the street, heading toward the library. It was clumsy and bulbous, and in the moonlight, it looked decrepit and old. But it was moving fast.

"We need to warn our friends," she said, crossing the threshold.

"No. It's too late!" he insisted, grabbing her hand and forcing her up the stairs. Then he pulled her along the sidewalk. "Hurry!"

"No!" she cried. "We have to tell them!"

"We don't have time." He shook his head as he looked fearfully in the direction of the bus. "Lilly, we can only save ourselves!"

"We have to try," she insisted.

"You don't get to be star quarterback by picking losers up off the field after they're tackled," he said. "You carry the ball to the infield. You look out for number one."

"Well . . . I don't," she said. She raised her chin. "I guess I'm not a star quarterback."

"Okay, fine, Lilly," he said, frowning at her. "You

stay here and get arrested. I'm outta here." He took off running down the street . . . just as the bus pulled up to the curb.

It was very long and rusty, with round bumpers and big, dirty white tires. An equally ancient man sat behind the wheel . . . and behind *him*, there were at least a dozen beefy men dressed in Mystery Meat gray uniforms.

Lilly's cell phone rang.

"Lilly?" It was Freekin.

"Freekin, I'm at the library! I'm at the seminar! We're in trouble!" she cried.

"Lilly, what did you do?" Freekin bellowed.

A spotlight surrounded Lilly and a huge circle of light blossomed around her.

"Stay where you are! This is the Society for the Prevention of Curiosity! You are under arrest!" a voice called out.

"Hurry, Freekin!" Lilly cried.

Chapter Nine:
In Which Our Hero
Acts Heroically!

"Lilly! I'm on my way!" Freekin shouted into the cell phone Pretty had "purchased" for him. He'd forgotten to turn the ringer back on; like the other kids, he put it on vibrate during school hours, and he could kick himself for missing Lilly's first call.

"Guys, Lilly went to the question-asking seminar at the library, and now she's in trouble," he told Pretty and

Scary. "So we have to save her. Scary, you transform into the super-secret spy plane and we'll fly over there."

The little phantom led the way out of the window and onto the tree branch, where he obediently transformed into the super-secret spy plane. Pretty and Freekin climbed inside, and they were off.

Sooner than one could say "autopsy," they hovered above the library. But no one was there! Not one single kid, no bus, nothing.

"Land," he told Scary.

The little spy plane descended among the maple trees. Freekin jumped out, dialing Lilly's cell phone number as he crept toward the entrance of the basement. Scary and Pretty trailed after him.

"Knock knock, oof," Pretty whispered, bumping into Freekin as he stared in horrified fascination at the scene in the basement.

No one sat among the jumbles of folding chairs; he saw a cardboard stand-up figure of himself and a whiteboard with questions written on it.

So now the Snickerings had rounded up the most Curious people in Snickering Willows . . . and Lilly.

"No," Freekin whispered. He thought a moment. "If they're arresting the kids for asking questions, they'll take them to the Juvenile Detention Facility. That's where they took me." He touched his fingers to his forehead. "This is a nightmare!"

"It okay, nice boy," Pretty promised him.

"*Zibu*," Scary ventured.

Freekin turned around and hurried up the basement steps. "Quick, Scary, morph into a spy plane," he said as he dialed Raven's number.

Less than ten minutes later, Freekin had organized a meeting with Steve, Raven, and Tuberculosis in Horatio Snickering Memorial Park, which was within walking distance of the Juvenile Detention Facility. Scary-plane touched down behind a large stand of trees, then changed into a corgi. Pretty growled at the statue of Horatio Snickering III and stuck out her tongue. Scary, still disguised as a corgi, woofed and defiantly passed some gas.

"Freekin," Raven greeted him. He was holding up a cell phone. "I just heard from Shadesse. The Society for the Prevention of Curiosity picked her up at the graveyard. She wasn't even at the meeting in the library."

"The graveyard," Steve said as he pushed along on his skateboard. Repeating something you didn't understand was a Snickering Willows way of asking a question, such as, *What was she doing in the graveyard?*

Raven nodded, looking stricken. "She was placing flowers on the graves of dead poets, in honor of the completion of my most recent poem. 'The bolts, the jolts, ten thousand volts . . .'" He trailed off.

"I *knew* it." Steve exhaled and balled his fists. "We should have warned everybody. Now they've been rounded up like—like *cattle*. They're going to be tried for Curiosity, found guilty, and sent off to work in the fermented fat factory until they die of old age. And then they'll be ground up into Mystery Meat. And it'll be all your fault, Freekin!"

"That is *not* going to happen," Freekin replied. Raven and Steve traded looks, and Freekin could practically read their minds: Steve was right. This was his fault.

"It's not going to happen," he repeated. "We'll go bust them out right now!"

"Lead the way," Steve said.

"Woof," Scary-corgi barked.

The group moved out across the snowy park. Tuberculosis fell in step beside Pretty. "You're Freekin's little sister," he said. "I haven't seen you around much."

"Oh, me so busy," she said, waving her hands.

"I'm still diggin' your dead bunny head," he added, gesturing to the decoration on her jumper.

Him so nice boy, Pretty thought.

"Me say thank you, doll," she replied.

"Maybe once this is over . . ." he began. "There's a dance . . ."

"Okeydoke, sure, whatever," she said, scooting past him to catch up with Freekin.

The Juvenile Detention Facility was one block across and one block down from the courthouse, the site of Freekin's trial for Curiosity. Freekin gazed up at the scudding clouds as they gathered behind the courthouse cupola, shrouding the face of the bone-white full moon as it hung in the sky.

Then the six stopped running and stood on the street opposite a large brick building with bars on all the windows. A large sign read, JUVENILE DETENTION FACILITY. At the top of the stairs, two burly men in police officer uniforms flanked the mayor of Snickering Willows and Principal Lugosi. More police officers stood in a semicircle at the bottom of the stairs, behind a white plastic barrier erected between them and a surging crowd of angry adults.

"My daughter is not a question asker!" That was Mr. Weezbrock, in his Mystery Meat union T-shirt, coat, and jeans.

"My sons are innocent!" a skinny little man bellowed. "Set them free!"

"We have to do something," Steve said. "But look at all those cops."

"When I was brought here, they drove me in through the back way. There's a big courtyard back there. If they've gathered up a bunch of kids, they're probably unloading them in the courtyard," Freekin said.

"Then let's go," Tuberculosis ventured.

Freekin took Pretty's hand, and the group moved stealthily through the crowd, crossing the street on the opposite side of the building, keeping to the shadows. A stately brick wall separated the courthouse grounds from the sidewalk. Freekin bent down and hoisted Pretty to the top of the wall.

"What can you see?" he asked her. He heard Steve's sharp intake of breath and realized he had asked a question aloud.

"Me see bus! And lotta kids," she answered. Her fangs clicked. "And bad Mystery Meaters! Me see Ms. Balonee! Mr. Spew! Mr. Flatterwonder!"

"Woof!" Scary-corgi barked.

"Those are the people in on the scheme," Freekin explained to the others. "Quick, Pretty, pull off my head and raise it up so I can see, too."

"Okeydoke," she said.

He held on to two thick vines of ivy while she bent over, laced her hands together beneath his chin, and yanked. His head popped off with a slick *thwwwack* and then he

had a headcam view as Pretty moved it in a slow arc.

Shuffling along behind the grim-faced brick building, a long line of kids was being led through the back entrance of the facility. There were a couple of adults, too—Mr. Cackle, who owned the Soul on Ice Skating Rink, and Mr. Moulder of the Wilting Fungus Day Spa.

Holding a bouquet of dead roses, Shadesse and another goth girl trudged behind the cheerleaders.

"Shadesse is walking with another goth girl," Freekin reported. "And there's Brian and Sam. And Brad Anderwater's there, too! They've got nearly every single kid in Snickering Willows!"

"They can keep Brad Anderwater," Steve said.

Then Freekin spotted Lilly, Deirdre, Janeece, and Molly, holding on to each other and looking very frightened.

"Lilly," he breathed.

"Grrr," Pretty growled softly.

"I feel the same way," he assured her. "We'll save her, Pretty. Put my head back on my body. I'm going to stop them."

"We're going, too," Steve said.

"No, you wait here," Freekin insisted. "You can't just walk in there. They'll arrest you, too."

"We already stood aside and let you handle it," Steve

reminded him. "And look how well that went." He glared at Freekin.

"Freekin has a point," Raven said. "He can't be permanently harmed. But we are mere simple, living, breathing humans."

"Fine," Steve snapped. "You wimpy goths can stay here if you want."

"You should *all* stay here," Freekin insisted.

———✷—✷—✷———

Pretty listened to the boys arguing, squared her shoulders, and gave her head a shake. Her ears danced and bobbed. She would prove to Freekin that she was his number one extra-special helper.

She handed Freekin's head to Tuberculosis, who was standing closest to her. Then she hopped off the wall. Snow began to fall as she trundled forward.

"Pretty, what are you doing?" Freekin said, his eyes sliding to the right to follow her as she scooted past Tuberculosis, who was still holding his head.

"Me extra-special helper," she announced. "Pretty makes a scene!"

"Let me get my head on straight! I'll come with you! Tuberculosis, put me together! Pretty, wait!"

"Arrrrooow!" Scary-corgi added, trotting beside Pretty.

But she was past waiting. Scary loyally jogged with

her as she trundled toward the courtyard. Just as she reached the wall, she spotted bad men pushing Brad Anderwater and some of the other kids into the Juvenile Detention Facility.

Steam rose from Pretty's head. Flames danced in all seven of her eyes. Smoke curled from her mouth.

"Pretty makes a scene!" she told the world.

Pretty was an old hand at setting sections of the Land of the Living on fire. She threw back her head and spread wide her arms (primarily for dramatic effect). Then she intoned the spell that would turn her into a terrifying, fire-spewing little monster:

"GAZEEKLIELKKEEEEEZA! KAZEELEELEELIO! AZEEELIILALALALALWAZU!"

Spouts of flames erupted from her eyes and her mouth. They blasted the courtyard wall, shattering it into smithereens of brick and sizzling vines of ivy that swooshed up into the air rather magnificently, if she did say so—and well out of harm's way, as far as Freekin's friends were concerned. Pretty wanted to scare the bad men into letting the kids go, but she didn't want to hurt anyone.

Well, she knew that she wasn't *supposed* to want that . . .

"Let's go!" Freekin shouted.

She turned to see Freekin, Raven, Steve, and Tuberculosis racing through the hole she had blasted in

the wall as the orderly line of prisoners disintegrated into clusters of kids grabbing onto each other. But the guards were pushing Lilly, Molly, Janeece, and Deirdre into the building to get them out of harm's way.

"Lilly, no!" Freekin bellowed, racing after her.

"Get him! It's Freekin Ripp!" one of the guards yelled.

Half a dozen guards started running after Freekin. Pretty trundled forward like a very small tank, throwing flame in her path to make a barrier between Freekin and the bad men. In the distance, fire engine sirens blared.

"Stop, or I'll—I'll throw my handcuffs at you!" one of the guards yelled at Pretty, shaking a pair of metal handcuffs at her.

Grinning broadly, she clacked her fangs. "Me so barbecuing, you so hottie," she warned the guard. Then she spewed fire in his direction—not too close, but forcing him to drop the cuffs and back off. He staggered backward, crashing into another guard, who grabbed him up and used him as a shield.

Pretty shot out more red-hot fiery breath . . . and something very unexpected happened: Skittering trails of yellow, orange, and scarlet flashed across the courtyard and ignited the bottom section of the brick building. The entire thing burst into flame! She didn't know that bricks

could burn. Pretty was so shocked, her jaw dropped. Scary, still in dog form at her side, began to yip.

"No, Pretty, stop!" Freekin screamed. "The building is on fire!"

And then *he* disappeared inside.

"Baroow woodiwoodi!" Scary-corgi protested.

"Aieee!" Pretty cried, so upset, she lost control and zoomed around in a circle like a gyroscope. This wasn't going at all the way she planned! *"Gazeeki woodiwoodi lali!"* she added, so stressed out that she broke into the only other foreign language she knew—Phantomese—instead of English. "Dearie me!" she cried. "Me so making boo-boo mess!"

Gentle Reader, you may recall that during all this excitement and chaos, Scary had been masquerading as a dog. Still in corgi shape, he barked as he looked left, right, and over his shoulder, ensuring that no one was watching him. Then he galloped into the shadows, transformed himself into a giant fire hose loaded with water, and aimed it at the building. The stream of water hissed and sizzled as it began to put out the flames. Scary divided himself into another hose and another until he looked more like a crazed many-headed serpent instead of a timid shape-shifting phantom.

"Good! Good!" Pretty screamed, clapping.

Scary could see that the fire around the door was going

out, so he glided along the courtyard to the left, spraying as he went. Pretty trailed after him, urging him on. But to his consternation, the fire was rising from the bottom floor to the upper levels, and he split himself into more hoses.

He was just about to turn into a rain cloud when he spotted Lilly, her three cheerleader friends, and Freekin through a second-story window. Lilly and the girls were doubled over, coughing; Freekin had just picked up a metal desk chair over his head and was rushing toward the window with it.

"*Woodiwoodi!*" Scary cried, and, without thinking, he immediately morphed into a tall fire ladder. Shooting from the ground to the windowsill, he used the tips of his wings to latch himself onto the outside of the window just as Freekin shattered the glass.

"Us saving you!" Pretty shouted, throwing open her arms. She started up the ladder, then zoomed back down, muttering to herself that she didn't want to get in the way of the human beings or else they might become *refried* beings. Up, down. She skittered in a circle, fangs clacking with anxiety.

"Hurry, Lilly!" Freekin shouted, helping her climb down the Scary-ladder.

"No, the others should go first," Lilly insisted. But she looked terrible, all sweaty and coughing and sick. She was

very pink, limp, and floppy like smoked turkey breast. It was obvious to Pretty that Yucky Lilly needed to get some fresh air into her lungs right this minute. Her three girlfriends weren't as bad off as she was.

"Come on, Yucky Lilly!" Pretty shouted from below. She clapped. "Here, girl, here, Lilly!"

Lilly could no longer put up much of a fight as Freekin helped her onto Scary's top rungs.

"Scary, Geronimooo!" Pretty commanded, grabbing onto the bottom of the "ladder" and pulling on it, and Scary slowly folded himself down, lowering a protesting Lilly into Pretty's outstretched arms. Lilly's legs dragged along the ground like the slime trails of snails as Pretty trundled her away to safety, staring down at her rival and thinking that Lilly was awfully brave. Pretty didn't want to say that she admired her . . .

. . . she really, really didn't want to say that,

. . . but she did.

"You so admire-y," she told Lilly.

"Take . . . care . . . of Freekin," Lilly murmured up at her.

Then Lilly fainted dead away.

This is Belle. Are you saying that she DIED?
This is Elvis. No way! She didn't die, did she?

Dear Belle and Elvis, you must wait and see.

Chapter Ten:
In Which Pretty Spills the Beans!

The fire was still raging, but Pretty figured Scary should stay and help Freekin and the cheerleaders instead of turning back into a fire hose.

"Go uppy," she told him.

"*Gazeekee zibu,*" Scary-ladder replied, extending back toward the window as Deirdre appeared with Freekin at the broken window, poised for her rescue.

"Okeydoke, Scary, you stay and help cheerleader girls," Pretty said, her attention on Scary as she caught sight of a firefighter wearing a mask walking toward her. "Here, Mr. Fireman," she said, holding out the unconscious Lilly. "Fix Lilly, okeydoke?"

The man bent down, took Lilly, and straightened. Lilly's cute little blue purse fell off her shoulder and landed on the ground. Pretty had retrieved it, preparing to give it to him, when he reached up a gloved hand to his face and lowered his mask.

"Thank you, Miss Pretty," he said in a familiar voice.

Pretty gasped as she stared at the rotting face of Horatio Snickering III. She made her face go slack. "Yes, master," she said. "Me obeying master."

He shook his head, tsk-tsking at her. "Naughty, naughty, Miss Pretty. I know you're not under my command any longer."

"Grrr," Pretty growled, abandoning her pretense as she trundled forward, preparing to make another scene.

"In my disguise as a firefighter, I have been observing your fine rescue attempt . . . and I have duly noted that your little friend Scary has changed himself into several things, including that ladder. Scary is a very clever shape-shifting phantom, but even he can't be a ladder *and* an extremely irritating undead boy at the same time.

Therefore, I also know that Freekin is not in a Terror-Induced Coma, as you assured me he was."

Pretty clacked her fangs and gave Lilly's purse the tiniest little gnaw. Oooooh, if she could get ahold of him, she would shred him!

"You thinking you so smarty-pants," she sneered at him. "Freekin hears you! Freekin knows you making more Curiosity! Him knows Henrietta Snickering is bad lady! Him knows everything!"

"Oh, really?" Horatio Snickering replied, raising a brow. "Well, thank you for letting *me* know that."

Oops. Pretty had a feeling she had just said way too much.

"Think of it, Miss Pretty," he continued. "If you had not tried to summon a boy monster from the Underworld, I would not have been able to cross back over. This is all your doing. You and you alone deserve the credit—or is it the blame?—for my victory over Snickering Willows! Ha ha ha!" He laughed. "Soon I'll have all the Curiosity I will ever need!"

"Grrr." Smoke rose from the top of her head.

"Ah-ah-ah," he cautioned, pointing to Lilly. "You wouldn't want to hurt this young lady, would you?"

Pretty didn't answer that. Once upon a time, she might have even said yes. After all, she was the yucky

human girl who had stolen Freekin's heart right from under Pretty's seven eyes. Pretty might even have fried her to get to Horatio Snickering III. But life in the Land of the Living had changed her. Mellowed her. Made her less monsterish.

"I can see that we need to be rid of Franklin once and for all before we proceed," Horatio Snickering went on. "Tell him to come to the fermented fat factory alone within the hour, or he will never see Lilly Weezbrock alive again."

He snapped his fingers.

With an ear-piercing squeal of brakes, his black limousine screeched into the chaotic courtyard. Horatio Snickering carried Lilly over to it. The back door swung open; Henrietta's skeleton-thin hands covered with enormous jeweled rings grabbed Lilly as Horatio practically threw her inside like a sack of Ultra Top Secret Ingredients. Then Mortadella the dog popped her scrawny little puff-topped head through the door.

"*Grrr-arf!*" Mortadella's beady eyes gleamed with canine malice.

"Bad doggie!" Pretty took a step toward the limousine.

"Careful, Miss Pretty," Horatio Snickering warned her. "We don't want anything to happen to Miss Weezbrock. Give Freekin my message. One hour."

He climbed backward into the limo. "Viggo, step on it," he ordered as he slammed the door.

The limo's wheels squealed like banshees as it circled and barreled between two fire trucks, narrowly missing two firefighters who were carrying a long hose. The vehicle raced out of the courtyard and flew down the street.

"No!" Pretty cried. "Bad, bad, bad!" She scooted around in a circle, then dizzily wobbled back to Scary as Deirdre, Molly, and Janeece all dropped to the ground from his sturdy little rungs and ran toward the hole in the wall. "Scary, *wazeelili*!" she screamed, waving her arms.

"*Zibu!*" Scary replied. Still ladder-shaped, he scooped up Pretty and hoisted her in the air. Slinging Lilly's purse over her shoulder, she scrabbled up his rungs in record time.

"Freekin! Help! Help!" she cried.

"Pretty?" Freekin stuck his head out the broken window.

"Freekin!" She clung to him. "Him so Horatio Snickering III! Bad man stealing Lilly! Him say, go to fermented fat factory right this minute young man!"

"*What?*" Freekin's face was a mask of horror. "He took her to the fermented fat factory?"

She nodded. "Oh, Freekin, me so sorry! C'mon now, we going—"

"Help!" someone yelled from inside the building. It was Brad Anderwater!

"Grrr. Him so refried being," Pretty pleaded, but she knew that leaving Brad Anderwater in the burning building was bad behavior.

"Help me!" Brad yelled more loudly, more desperately, more refried-ly.

"Gotta go," Freekin told her, and he dashed back into the fiery building.

"Him so hero." Pretty sighed.

Found him!

Freekin located Brad Anderwater slumped down the hall and to the right, in the corner of a locked Juvenile Detention cell. The other cells he passed on the way to Brad were open and empty. Without a moment's hesitation, he slung his unconscious archrival over his shoulder and headed back toward the room with the broken window, where he knew Scary would be waiting. But the hall leading to the room was raging with flames.

He went down another way, to discover that the door he had used to enter the building was blocked as well.

So he twisted and turned and backtracked with Brad on his back until he burst through the front door of the Juvenile Detention Facility, on the same spot where the mayor and chief of police stood side by side, still facing the crowd of angry parents. Now there were fire trucks, firefighters, ambulances, paramedics, and a lot of very frightened adults.

"Here," Freekin said as two paramedics flew up the stairs. Then Freekin laid Brad onto the stretcher they were carrying, while his nemesis stirred and pointed his finger at Freekin.

"Freekin Ripp! He's the one who started the fire! I saw him do it!" Brad said, coughing.

"He's the leader of the Curiosity underground!" someone shouted from the crowd. "Get him!"

Freekin turned to race back into the burning building. But a firefighter with a kid over his shoulder blocked his way. He veered to the right and darted along the face of the building, hoping to circle to the back. *Ba-zing!* A bullet whizzed past his ear. *Ka-zoing!* A second one just missed his cheek. The bullets wouldn't harm him, but they might shoot part of him off, and that would slow him down for sure.

He ran faster, bracing himself for another shot. Instead he heard shouts, lots of them.

"Get him!" someone bellowed.

"Freekin, where's my son?" That was a parent. A parent, *asking a question!*

"Stop, Ripp!"

He turned his head. The parents had broken through

the barricades. They were swarming around the cops, their faces contorted with rage and hatred as they cut off his exit route. They came at him like a swarm of stinging bees.

Freekin hung a U-ie and ran away so fast, he thought his legs would detach any second.

Pretty hurried over to Scary, who was still transformed into a ladder, and squinted upward into the smoky steam. Thanks to the firefighters lined up with real hoses spraying gobs of water at the Juvenile Detention Facility, the fire was guttering out. But Freekin hadn't appeared at the window with Brad Anderwater, and what was that shouting she heard on the other side of the building?

"Knock knock, Scary," she called, trundling out of sight around the corner of the building. Scary folded himself up, and when he was sure no one was looking, he turned into his normal phantom shape and joined her.

"Scary is super-secret spy plane," Pretty commanded, and Scary immediately transformed. Pretty climbed inside, and they silently rose into the air, beneath the glowing full moon. She nervously tapped her fingers on Lilly's purse. Together the two monsters soared above the building, observing the mob running down the street.

"You so flying," Pretty urged as they swooped ahead

of the crowd. Who were they so mad at? Who were they chasing?

She could kind of guess.

"Keeping going," she told Scary, who bobbed his nose in reply. They soared along the towers and spires of Snickering Willows, following the mob, but eventually the people stopped running and started going off in all directions. They had lost Freekin.

"Okay!" Pretty cried, clapping. "Us going to fat factory."

"*Gazeeka?*" Scary asked.

"Where?" Pretty thought a moment. She had no idea where the fermented fat factory was.

They circled for a few minutes. Pretty was aware that their time was ticking away. She started gazing out the window, looking for Freekin's friends. But it was dark, and the smoke obscured her view, and she suddenly got very panicky. What if Freekin went off to save Lilly by himself and something bad happened? What if Horatio Snickering III ground Freekin into Mystery Meat?

She burst into tears. And then she shrieked and jabbed her finger at the town below.

"Freekin's house! Freekin's house!" she cried. "Geronimooooo, Scary!"

Scary plummeted to earth. Pretty flung herself down

141

the steps and slithered up the tree branch into Freekin's room. She zoomed over to his study desk and opened his computer files, searching for the phone numbers of his friends. Finally she spied a desktop folder labeled NUMBERS & ADDYS, and she double-clicked it open. The first number on the list was for Steve.

"Got 'em!" she told Scary. She snapped her fingers. "Phone!"

Scary immediately transformed into a cell phone. Pretty dialed the number.

"Steve, Steve!" she screamed to the ring tone. She made herself wait for the connection.

"Hello!"

"Me so Pretty! Freekin, him go to the fermented fat factory!"

"Okay," Steve said. "Well then I should probably meet him there."

"Yes, yes, yes!" she cried, bouncing on her tentacles.

"Raven and Tuberculosis are with me. We're on our way. But we don't know where it is!" Steve said.

"Um . . ." She blanched. "Me not knowing."

"I don't know, either. Hold on."

She drummed her tentacles on Freekin's desk. Then she realized she could do a search on Freekin's computer! She typed in FERMENTED FAT FACTORY and held her breath.

The computer whirled for a moment.

NO MATCH FOUND.

She whimpered. She tried several variations.

NO MATCH FOUND.

"They don't know where it is, either," Steve said on the Scary-phone.

Her fangs clacked. "Okeydoke," she said. "Me say bye now, later."

"Let's check in with each other in a few," he said. Then he hung up.

"Scary, me so desperation," Pretty said, tears rolling down her cheeks. She paced back and forth, her kitties trailing after her, batting at her tentacles.

This was all her fault. She had tried to summon a boy so she could hurt Freekin's feelings and look at what had happened instead. If only she could fix what she had done, go back in time and . . .

And . . .

Her eyes flashed and zoomed. Her ears flapped as she bounced like a pogo stick on her tentacles. "Me summoning someone else," she informed Scary. "Us going to graveyard right this minute young man!"

"*Zibu*," Scary said.

Chapter Eleven:
In Which Pretty Summons an Unlikely Ally!

Through the dark and spooky night, Scary flew Pretty to the graveyard and landed not far from Sweeny Burton's empty grave. Pretty hopped out and Scary turned back into himself. Pretty was very nervous, but she was determined to go through with her daring plan: to summon Lord Grym-Reaper from the Afterlife and ask him for his help. It was a terrifying idea—enough to

put her in a coma—but she was from the Afterlife, and she couldn't think of anyone more powerful than the dreaded Lord of the Dead anywhere, on either side of the veil of life.

Lord Grym-Reaper was the only member of the Afterlife Commission who could cross over to the Land of the Living and back again. Human beings never remembered seeing him when they died, but he was always there. He threw back his robe and looked upon them, and then they crossed over and woke up in the Afterlife.

Dear Reader, you certainly do remember that Pretty is a very little monster, and despite her apparent boldness, the Afterlife Commission intimidated her. They were quite powerful, after all.

She had no idea if her spell would work and, if it did, what Lord Grym-Reaper would do when he realized she had summoned him. But she would do *anything* to save her Freekin.

So she was uncharacteristically quiet when she cleared her throat and began her spell, managing only to whisper, so quietly that not even Scary could hear her. She shut her eyes tightly and fidgeted with Lilly's purse.

"GAZEEKELILI GAZEEBA, WAHOULA," she murmured.

Nothing happened. She tried again.

"GAZEEKELILI GAZEEBA, WAHOULA."

Maybe the snowy ground beneath her feet shifted a bit.

"GAZEEKELILI GAZEEBA—"

"Oooooooh," Scary said.

Pretty opened her eyes.

Before her stood a hearse. A skeleton in a chauffeur's uniform sat in the driver's seat, and in the back, Pretty saw the silhouette of Lord Grym-Reaper.

Then she grabbed Scary's hand and the two stumbled toward the hearse. Scary was quivering from head to toe.

"*Woodiwoodi,*" he whispered. "*Woodiwoodiwoodi.*"

"It okay," Pretty soothed him, but she had no idea if that was true.

The hearse window unrolled and the two Underworlders beheld Lord Grym-Reaper in his hooded robe; they could see nothing of his face but his sinister black eyes, fixed on them.

"Um," Pretty said uneasily. "Me say hi, sir."

"It was *you* who summoned me?" he asked. Each syllable was like an ice cube dropped down the back of Pretty's jumper. "I must remember to get my hearing checked. I could have sworn it was, well, you know." He paused and then whispered, "The Man upstairs."

"Me so sorry to disturb sir." She bobbed low on her

tentacles. Scary nodded in agreement and cast his eyes toward the ground.

"Well, it's too late for apologies now. I already made the trip all the way over here. You might as well tell me what it is you want," said Lord Grym-Reaper.

"Oh, we having many big problems, Lord Grym-Reaper, many, many, many," she began earnestly.

His face brightened. "People don't know this about me, but I like good gossip as much as the next guy," he said as he patted the seat next to him. "Come inside," he said as the hearse door opened by itself.

So Pretty crawled inside and sat beside the imposing being, swinging her tentacles as the whole long story poured out of her.

"So Franklin was chased off by a mob, and his one true love—the girl he must kiss—has been taken to a fermented fat factory?"

"Uh-huh, yes sirree," she said. Her ponytail ears bobbed as she nodded. "Horatio Snickering III, him so undead, him taking her!"

"What?" The dread lord was shocked. *"Another person has returned to the Land of the Living from the Afterlife?"*

She nodded.

"I will not permit this!" Lord Grym-Reaper decreed.

"We will leave immediately—"

"Pretty!" a voice cried from beyond the gates of the cemetery. It was Tuberculosis.

"Uh-oh, Freekin's goth buddy," Pretty whispered. "Him have so many friends."

"Send him away at once," the dread lord commanded, grabbing his hood and pulling it over his head to conceal his features. "No human may look upon me and live."

"Hey, Pretty!" Steve was there, too. And Raven. They were climbing over the iron fence!

"Stop them," Lord Grym-Reaper ordered her. "It is not yet their time to meet me."

Pretty had an idea. She opened Lilly's purse and peered inside. Assured that she could pull off her plan, she smiled hopefully at Lord Grym-Reaper. "Please, they helping, please," she said. "Pretty fixes things."

Less than a minute later, Steve, Raven, and Tuberculosis were gathered around Lord Grym-Reaper's limousine. The chauffeur's tinted window was up, concealing the skeleton driver from their view.

"I can't believe that you won a car in a beauty pageant," Steve said. "And that in the middle of all this confusion, they delivered it to you! But it's perfect timing. They're rounding up the adults and people are starting to ask questions and it's a huge mess. We can use some wheels."

"Yeah, we've been looking for you everywhere," Tuberculosis added. "And I, for one, *can* believe that you won the Miss Snickering Willows Mall beauty pageant." He smiled first at Pretty, lingering on her face, and then peered in through the half-open passenger window at Lord Grym-Reaper as well. "And that you won first runner-up, Miss Reaperina. It's very nice to meet you."

"Her Grimelda," Pretty corrected him. "*Grimelda* Reaperina."

The dread lord remained silent. Pretty thought he was beautiful. She had hurriedly but skillfully applied a thick coat of makeup to his ghostly face, complete with blue eye shadow, rosy red cheeks, and scarlet lips. Scary had transformed into a wig of thick black curls and a glittering tiara. Pretty was so grateful that Lord Grym-Reaper had agreed with her scheme to disguise him.

"So, us taking Grimelda home, you keeping car, you looking for kids," Pretty said.

Lord Grym-Reaper shifted in his seat. Pretty grabbed his hand, hidden inside his robe. "Okeydoke, Grimelda my dear?" Lord Grym-Reaper sort of growled.

Nestled among the crags and precipices of the Snarkshire Mountains, the fermented fat factory disgorged stinky puffs of oily smoke as it burbled away in the night. Freekin had run all the way there; since he was undead, he never got tired, and he could run very fast. By the time he got there, his left foot was flapping again, but he had made it.

The fermented fat factory was built of bricks coated with decades of congealed fat secretions, which had rotted and attracted hundreds of thousands of ants, cockroaches, and rats. The creatures swarmed all over the bricks, seemingly able to defy gravity.

Two enormous iron doors hung open in invitation, and Freekin went through them, then down, down, down into the bowels of the factory to the dark, dreary cavern that he had seen on the DVD in Henrietta Snickering's mansion.

Lilly was twenty feet away, dressed in a prison jumpsuit of Mystery Meat gray. Her lovely blond hair hung in sweaty, oily lanks around her shoulders. She was standing on a stepladder, bent over an old-fashioned cast-iron cauldron, stirring the barf-colored contents with a large stick, and her face was drawn and tired.

"Lilly!" he shouted, run-flapping, run-flapping toward her.

"Freekin!" She straightened. "Freekin, no, it's a trap!"

"Hello, Franklin," said Horatio Snickering III as he

and his diabolical great-great-great-great-niece Henrietta stepped from the shadows, placing themselves between Freekin and Lilly. Henrietta was wearing all white, like a nurse, with long rubber gloves that stretched past her bony elbows. Her evil little dog, Mortadella, squirmed in her arms and yipped at Freekin.

"You're finally here. It's very nice to meet you, young man." He smiled, and a maggot dropped out of his mouth. He flicked it away with a casual air.

"Indeed," Henrietta agreed. "It's nice to meet you, but it will be even nicer to turn you into Mystery Meat."

"You can't do that," Lilly said. "You won't do that!"

"Viggo, make sure no one else shows up," Horatio Snickering said to the shadows. Viggo appeared, his buggy eyes gleaming as he smiled unpleasantly at Freekin.

"And Miss Weezbrock," Horatio added, "do be quiet, or we will have to gag you."

Horatio pulled a rotten handkerchief from his pocket and showed it to Lilly. Lilly clamped her mouth shut and stared at Freekin with pure and utter misery.

"Your little girlfriend has proven to be quite Curious, which will make her quite delicious," Henrietta said. "She couldn't stop asking questions: 'Where are you taking me? Why are you doing this? Are you going to kill me?' And my personal favorite: 'Freekin, where are you?'"

Freekin glared at the Snickerings. "I'm here, Lilly," he told her, then he shifted his gaze back to the Snickerings. "You told me to come if I wanted to save Lilly. So now what?"

"You will take her place, of course," Horatio Snickering III said grandly. "You will step into the cauldron and boil away."

"No!" Lilly cried, her eyes and mouth going wide with terror.

"If I do that, will you let her go?"

Henrietta threw back her head and laughed. Mortadella barked and snapped her teeth at Freekin. "Let her go. If you mean, will we take her back to Snickering Willows, the answer is yes."

"Then we have a deal," Freekin said.

"Freekin, don't do it," Lilly begged him. "They're lying. It won't save me. I heard them talking in the limo on the way here. They thought I was unconscious. They said that sooner or later, all your friends will wind up here. The mayor is in on the plot. And so is the chief of police."

"That's true, we did say that," Horatio agreed. "But I promise, Freekin, we'll take her back to town tonight and leave her alone until at least tomorrow morning."

He smiled his jaggedy smile. "Mr. Ripp, if you

please, join Miss Weezbrock on her little step stool. Miss Weezbrock, you will then have the honor of pushing him in."

Back in the graveyard, Lord Grym-Reaper made sure Tuberculosis and the others couldn't see through the tinted windows of the driver's section of his "limo" before he consented to let them use it. Then, as soon they drove away on their mission to rescue the people of Snickering Willows, Scary changed from a tiara and a curly black wig into the super-secret spy plane, and Pretty and Lord Grym-Reaper climbed aboard. Scary shot into the sky, wondering if the dread lord remembered that he was wearing a lot of makeup. He had made no effort to wipe it off, and he looked very, very weird.

"To the fermented fat factory, and hurry," Lord Grym-Reaper told him.

Scary flew as fast as he could, scaring the daylights out of a passing swarm of bats.

"You two care very much for this undead boy," Lord Grym-Reaper observed as they sped along. "And so do his many human friends. He was correct when he told us that he had quite a good life before he was cut down. I am truly impressed."

"Yay," Pretty said, batting her lashes at him.

Then his face hardened. His thin red lips pursed together tightly, like a cut.

"But as for the Snickerings . . . they have much to answer for."

"Yay," Pretty said again.

In the distance, a single plume of tallow-colored smoke twisted ominously from the jumbled silhouette of the fermented fat factory.

"Zoom, please," Pretty begged Scary.

At the factory, Freekin faced Lilly, possibly for the last time. He could smell her scent even though it mingled with smoke, sweat, fat, and grime. It was the most wonderful smell in the world.

Lilly gazed up at him with tears in her big beautiful blue eyes. "I can't believe it's going to end like this, Freekin. Maybe after you're boiled down, I can strain you and put you back together like a big meatball."

"Look at that," Horatio Snickering III said to Henrietta. "True love blossoms in the face of tragedy. The girl has lost her head."

Lost her head, Freekin thought. *Of course!*

Freekin gazed hard at Lilly. "Maybe I'm the one who's lost his head. Over you, Lilly." Then he lowered his voice so that only she could hear. "Remember at the football

game, when they used my head as a fake football? I lost my head a lot."

She nodded. "You did. You lost it all the time." Her brows shot up. *"Oh."*

They shared a moment. They were in sync. They were . . . *ready.*

"Enough romance!" Henrietta shrieked. "Push him in!"

But Lilly had gotten his message. She knew just what to do.

"Good-bye, Freekin!" she cried dramatically, throwing the back of her hand across her forehead. "Alas! Woe is me! I will always miss you!"

Horatio and Henrietta cackled with glee. They embraced each other . . . and in that moment, when they were distracted, Lilly reached down, yanked off Freekin's head, and threw it as hard as she could at the diabolical pair!

"Yeeeeee-ha!" Freekin yelled as his head crashed into Henrietta Snickering's skull with a resounding thwack. The momentum slammed her into Horatio Snickering, who staggered backward, nearly losing his balance . . . but not quite. He caught Freekin's head and held it against his moss-covered sternum, over his crab apple heart.

Freekin blinked. "Run, Lilly!" he told her.

"Mortadella, attack!" Henrietta shouted as the

loathsome little creature popped out of her arms. The dog flew across the floor and sprang at Lilly, aiming for her throat.

"Freekin!" Lilly screamed as his headless body pulled her down into a squat. Mortadella sailed over Lilly's head and skittered along the tile floor.

"Arfarfarfarfarfarfarfarfarfarfarfarfarfarfarfarfarfarf arfarfarfarfarfarfarfarfarfarfarfarfarfarfarfarfarfarfarf arfarfarfarfarfarfarfarfarfarfarfarfarfarfarfarfarfarf." Mortadella yipped as she slid back around and headed back toward Freekin and Lilly.

Lilly broke Freekin's arm off at the wrist. His bicep flexed and he bent his elbow into a boomerang shape.

"Throw me at the dog!" Freekin's head called to her.

As much as Lilly hated hurting animals, she knew she had to do it.

As a cheerleader, she had watched a lot of football passes, and now she imagined the ball—or Freekin's arm—shooting down the infield. It arched into the fetid air of the cavern and went wide.

"Arfarfarfarfarfarfarfarfarfarfarfarfarfarfarfarfarfarf arfarfarfarfarfarfarfarfarfarfarfarfarfarfarfarfarfarfarf arfarfarfarfarfarfarfarfarfarfarfarfarfarfarfarfarfarf." Mortadella yipped, zooming after it.

"Try again!" Freekin shouted from across the cavern.

"Shut up!" Horatio yelled at him.

"Don't you talk to him like that!" Lilly cried.

With a mighty *crack!* Lilly tore Freekin's other arm free and aimed at Horatio. That arm went wide as well, and Horatio caught it, raising it over his head.

"You'll have to do better than that, my dear!" he challenged her.

Lilly went for Freekin's upper leg next and hurtled it at Henrietta. It slammed into her and landed her on her bottom.

"Stop her! She's ruining everything!" Henrietta cried.

"Henrietta, for heaven's sake, calm down and hold this." He picked up Freekin's head and lofted it up and down like a ball. "We'll just dump him in like chicken pieces."

"Arfarfarfarfarfarfarfarfarfarfarfarfarfarfarf arfarfarfarfarfarfarfarfarfarfarfarfarfarfarfarfarfarf arfarfarfarfarfarfarfarfarfarfarfarfarfarfarfarfarf." Mortadella barked triumphantly, as she leaped back onto Lilly's stepladder again.

Lilly shrieked and fell backward, catching herself from slipping into the cauldron. The lip of the huge pot was very hot, but she stayed put, raising up her feet to keep them out of Mortadella's reach.

"Help!" Lilly shouted. "Please, somebody, help us!"

"No one is coming, my dear," Henrietta said, grinning maniacally. "Just jump into the cauldron. Make it easier on us."

"Grrrrrrrrrrrrrrrrrrrrrrrrr," Mortadella growled, as she danced on her back legs and snapped at Lilly's toes.

"The evil little dog grabbed Freekin's torso and other leg between her teeth, and gave them a fierce shake.

Horatio and Henrietta laughed so hard they could hardly move "Fetch him, dear!" Henrietta cried. "All of him."

As Lilly watched in horror, Horatio drew closer to the cauldron and held Freekin's head above the bubbling fermented fat, pausing dramatically.

"I'm sure Freekin's intense Curiosity will prove to be very tasty," he told Lilly, leering at her.

"Freekin, no!" Lilly pleaded.

Henrietta touched her hands to her face. "We've never actually *murdered* anyone before," she said anxiously.

"*You* haven't," Horatio corrected her, with a very terrible smile.

Chapter Twelve:
In Which Our Story Concludes!
(Almost!)

"Wheeeeeeeeeeeee!" Pretty screamed as the Scary-plane blasted through the brick wall of the fermented fat factory, then through the floor, and spiraled down, down into the cavern. Transforming into a fearsome, swooping pterodactyl with Pretty and Lord Grym-Reaper (who still had on his makeup) on his back, Scary cawed and clacked his sharp beak.

As she screamed and clung to his head, Pretty wrapped her tentacles around his feathers and pushed off him like a giant spring, shooting herself straight at Horatio Snickering. She grabbed Freekin's head out of his hands and sprung back onto Scary. Then she dove down again and grabbed his torso and leg. Lord Grym-Reaper got started on putting him back together.

"Wheeeeeeeeeee!" she shrieked again.

"Stop it, stop at once!" Horatio shouted.

"Us so fixing Freekin!" Pretty cried, as the plane dipped and dove, and she gathered up all the Freekin bits and the dread lord of the dead jammed them together in rapid fire fixing mode—hipbones, legbones, thighbones, until Freekin was fully freaked-up once more!

This is Belle! Wow, that is so cool!

This is Elvis. Freekin rocks!

Next Pretty hurtled herself at Mortadella instead—and missed.

"Mortadella, come to Mommy!" Henrietta cried, bending over and opening her arms. "I'll protect you!"

But the little dog scampered into the shadows, whining and growling, her toenails clicking against the tiles.

Horatio Snickering III stared up at Lord Grym-Reaper, who gently sat Freekin down.

"I am the dread lord of the undead. It was I who cut you down when your time came, was it not?"

"Yes, sir," Horatio Snickering said humbly, dropping to his knees. "And I only came back here because things were in such disarray. I was about to finish up and come back, honest—"

"Silence!" Lord Grym-Reaper thundered. Horatio Snickering lowered his head, and Lord Grym-Reaper turned to Henrietta.

"What have you to say for yourself? Do you wish this to be your time?"

"Oh, please, Ms. Death . . . or should I say Mr. Death," Henrietta began, making a deep, shaky curtsy. "I didn't mean to cause any harm. I was just trying to make a living—"

"A living, out of the dead?" Lord Grym-Reaper shouted at her. "Out of Franklin Ripp, who is here with the permission of the Afterlife Commission, while your ancestor is not? How dare you!" He opened his hand. "Once I close this fist, your heart will stop beating." He bent his fingers.

"Her bad lady, eat her eyeballs," Pretty advised.

"*Woodiwoodi,*" Scary-pterodactyl murmured fretfully, shutting his eyes so that he wouldn't have to look.

"No!" Henrietta cried, raising her hands. "Please! I'll do

anything! I'll—I'll confess!" she said, grabbing her chest.

His fingers were almost touching each other. "You'll confess. And you will reveal the secret of Mystery Meat."

"No, please," Horatio Snickering III whispered, but he quickly shut his mouth and cast his gaze downward.

"Yes, if it will save my life," Henrietta promised.

"She has a DVD that tells the whole story," Freekin said, with both his arms around Lilly. Her head was on his chest and her hands were bright red. "Make her show it in public, at the school gym."

"I'll do it, I promise," Henrietta said.

"Very well." Lord Grym-Reaper opened his hand. "The only reason you are still alive at this moment is that you have not looked upon my true face."

"Him so makeup," Pretty said helpfully.

"Scary, descend, please," Lord Grym-Reaper ordered.

Pretty, Freekin, and Scary searched the entire fermented fat factory for Viggo and Mortadella. But in all the hubbub, they had left the building—of that, the three were completely positive.

"Don't worry about them," Lord Grym-Reaper assured the friends. "I will find them when it's time."

"Oh, my poor baby!" Henrietta wailed.

Ignoring her, Lord Grym-Reaper turned to Pretty.

"Make a scene, my dear little monster friend."

"Yes sirree, my dear!" Pretty screamed with glee.

While Pretty burned every single last brick of the fermented fat factory to the ground, Scary flew everyone else outside. They watched as the evil building went up in smoke, and Freekin knew it was only a matter of time before the Mystery Meat factory itself was gone, too.

Lilly put her head on Freekin's head.

"It's really over," Lilly whispered, taking Freekin's hand. "You ended it." They turned to each other, smiling. They drew closer, closer . . .

Clink!

A piece of metal fell from a pile of ashes, startling everyone . . . and interrupting the kiss.

"Let's go home," Freekin said.

"Scary, please take us to the graveyard," Lord Grym-Reaper told the little phantom. "And then it will be time for us to say farewell . . . for now."

In the graveyard, Freekin faced Lord Grym-Reaper as the imperious being stood with a trembling Horatio Snickering III at his side. Pretty held Freekin's hand very tight. Scary cooed beside him.

Lilly stood a distance away, hands in the pocket of her coat, trembling with cold and fear. It was as if she had finally realized what had really happened, and Freekin hoped she wouldn't be too afraid to hang out with him anymore.

Lord Grym-Reaper's blazing gaze moved up, down, taking in the full measure of the undead boy before him. Then he did something he rarely did, for he was a dread lord indeed: He smiled.

"I'm impressed with you, Freekin. You're a most entertaining lad. If things don't work out here, it would be nice to see you come back home."

Freekin swallowed. He didn't especially want Lord Grym-Reaper to look forward to his return "home." "Thanks," he said.

"Pretty, you were wise to call for me. It was very brave of you. I will cloud Miss Weezbrock's mind so that she forgets she ever saw me, Horatio Snickering III, and Scary. We three are things not meant for mortal eyes."

"Yes sir," she said. "Um, me so thanking you, hope you had a lovely time, come back soon."

He laughed, a low, deep timbre that vibrated through the earth. Then he pointed his long arm at Lilly and snapped his fingers. Remaining upright, she closed her eyes.

"Come along, Horatio," Lord Grym-Reaper said.

Horatio Snickering III took his place beside Lord Grym-Reaper.

Then they vanished. Just like that. No fanfare, no *poof* of otherworldly mist. They were just . . . gone.

Pretty, Freekin, and Scary stood for a moment in utter silence. Then they burst into whoops of joy.

"We did it, you guys!" Freekin cried. "We saved the town, and Lilly, and we solved the mystery of the Mystery Meat!" He cheered and threw up his hands over his head. Up they soared, up, up, high into the sky.

"High five! We so rocking!" Pretty screamed as she zoomed around in a circle.

"Zibu!" Scary added, transforming into a catcher's mitt and catching both of Freekin's hands as the three of them plummeted to earth.

"We're so rocking," Freekin said, laughing, as he took back his hands and attached them onto his wrists. "All three of us, together. Pretty, Freekin, and Scary."

Lilly's eyes slowly opened. "Where am I?" she asked. "What happened?"

"Nothing much," Freekin said, winking at Pretty—and Scary, who had changed back into a Welsh corgi.

Pretty burst into giggles and Scary bounded around her, barking with joy.

Epilogue:
In Which Freekin Receives
His Hero's Reward!

It was the night of the Nonspecific Winter Holiday Dance. Lilly's dad had totally warmed up to Freekin after he found out that the "Dead Boy" saved his daughter's life. He even paid for the dance tickets *and* the limousine. On the big night, Freekin and Lilly shared their limousine with Raven and Shadesse and Pretty and Tuberculosis. For Tuberculosis had indeed asked Pretty to the dance, and what could she say? She already had a dress. Besides, he looked kind of cute in his all-black tuxedo.

Scary had disguised himself as some dead roses to circle Pretty's ponytail ears. Tuberculosis had bought her a corsage of black roses—how cool was that?!—and told her that he liked the red velvet dead bunny head on her gown.

The two couples paused on the threshold of the dreamy gym, which was decorated with silver and blue question marks hanging from the ceiling. Lilly had worn a dark blue dress that matched her dark blue eyes.

"Geeeee," Scary whispered in Pretty's hair, and the two Underworlders took a moment to reflect on their amazing adventures and good fortune. They had been best friends for thousands and millions of years, and here they were together, in a beautiful waking dream.

Henrietta Snickering had already been tried for Evil and found guilty of shipping off the Curious citizens of Snickering Willows to the fermented fat factory for generations. She was sentenced to life in prison, and the revolting recipe for Mystery Meat was published in the *Daily Snicker* and broadcast on TV. The hideous secret of the Snickerings was a secret no longer.

Her lackeys—Ms. Balonee, Mr. Spew, and Mr. Flatterwonder—were in prison, and the mayor and the

police chief were awaiting trial. The law against Curiosity was declared null and void, and there was dancing in the streets. Naturally, all those arrested for Curiosity were let go, and Curiosity seminars and classes sprang up all over town.

Viggo and Mortadella stayed gone, although there were rumors of a crazed dog arfing and yipping as she chased a hunchbacked man over the quivering moors of Snorting Cypresses, the next town over.

Freekin was declared the hero of the hour and the savior of Snickering Willows, and as he and Lilly led the way into the dance, all the students turned and began to applaud. Everyone was wearing a button that read, ? GENERATION RULES!

"Here he is, Freekin Ripp!" called Mr. Karloff, the football coach, from the little stage where the DJ was set up.

"Freekin! Freekin!" the kids and teachers shouted. They clapped and stomped their feet. Steve, Hal, and Otter waved. Sam, Brian, and Jessie said, "Woo woo woo!" in the way of jocks. Janeece and Molly blew kisses at Lilly.

Freekin turned to Pretty and Scary. "Thanks again, you guys," he murmured. "You're the best friends I could ever hope to have."

The word *friends* hurt Pretty's feelings a little, because she still wanted to be Freekin's *girl*friend. There was a big difference. But she had agreed to do anything she could to save her Freekin, and if that meant letting Yucky Lilly have him, she would.

For now, anyway.

"Us good friends," she agreed. "Best friends!"

"Zibu," Scary whispered softly, giving her a knowing little smile. She smiled back.

Then Pretty hugged Lilly and took Tuberculosis's hand. "We so dancing," she told him. "La la la!"

"Come on up here, Freekin!" the coach urged him. "And Lilly, too. We have something for you."

Lilly looked at Freekin, and he returned her gaze. Then they walked together past all the cheering people in the gym and climbed onto the stage. The question mark decorations turned and glittered, and Lilly's blond hair gleamed.

At a signal from Coach Karloff, Deirdre walked from the back of the stage. She was carrying two golden crowns, also decorated with question marks, on a little purple pillow. She held it up to Coach Karloff, who picked up the smaller, daintier of the two crowns and held it above Lilly's head.

"I give you Lilly, Queen of the Nonspecific Winter

Holiday Dance!" he announced, and placed the crown on her head. Lilly's eyes glittered as she excitedly covered her mouth with her hands.

"And I give you Freekin, your king!" the coach added. Then he placed the larger crown on Freekin's head.

"Wow," Freekin murmured to Lilly as they waved at everyone. Below, on the gym floor, Pretty was bouncing up on her tentacles, cheering and waving at him. Scary briefly popped a wing and waved at him, too.

"Wow," Lilly echoed. She took both his hands in hers and faced him. "Wow, Freekin Ripp."

Kiss her, he told himself. *Kiss her now.*

But he didn't.

This is Belle. Uncle Chris, you have got to be kidding me.

This is Elvis. I think he is kidding us.

Dear Girls and Gentle Reader, I would never kid you on a matter as serious as this. For as you recall, Freekin's one requirement for remaining in the Land of the Living for the rest of his natural unlife was to kiss Lilly Weezbrock. But he didn't.

Instead, he let *her* kiss *him.*

"You kissed me," Freekin whispered.

"I kissed you," she said. "Now kiss me back."

A cheer rose up all around the gym, and the music swelled. And Freekin thought . . . although he wasn't positive . . . that his heart might have beat just then.

I get to stay, he thought. He smiled over Lilly's shoulder at Pretty and Scary. *We get to stay.*

And then he kissed Lilly back. The way heroes kiss heroines. The way true love kisses. The way that makes life worth living.

And so we leave them together, kissing. And maybe Pretty shed a tear, but she was cheered up by Tuberculosis, who told her she was the prettiest girl in the room, and Scary-tiara gave her a tender little butterfly kiss on the top of her head.

Awwww! This is Belle. This is such a happy ending!

This is Elvis! That is soooooo sweet!

Indeed. It is sweet. But it's certainly not an ending.

It's a beginning.